OUT OF THE MARTIAN JUNGLE

Imagine, if you can, a bald-faced hornet of your Earthly experience grown to the size of a prize Hereford bull, and you will have same faint conception of the winged monster that bore down upon me.

Frightful jaws in front and a mighty, poisoned sting behind made my relatively puny long-sword seem a pitiful defense indeed. Nor could I hope to escape the lightning-live movements or hide from those myriad facet eyes which covered three-fourths of the hideous head, permitting the creature to see in all directions at once.

To flee was useless, even if it had ever been to my liking to turn my back upon a danger; so I stood my ground, my only hope to die as I had always lived—fighting.

THE WARLORD OF MARS

Edgar Rice Burroughs

A Del Rey Book

BALLANTINE BOOKS • NEW YORK

A Del Rey Book
Published by Ballantine Books

ISBN 0-345-27836-4

Mnaufactured in the United States of America

First U.S. Printing: March 1963
Eighteenth U.S. Printing: September 1982

CONTENTS

THE WARLORD OF MARS

ON THE RIVER ISS

IN THE shadows of the forest that flanks the crimson plain by the side of the Lost Sea of Korus in the Valley Dor, beneath the hurtling moons of Mars, speeding their meteoric way close above the bosom of the dying planet, I crept stealthily along the trail of a shadowy form that hugged the darker places with a persistency that proclaimed the sinister nature of its errand.

For six long Martian months I had haunted the vicinity of the hateful Temple of the Sun, within whose slow-revolving shaft, far beneath the surface of Mars, my princess lay entombed—but whether alive or dead I knew not. Had Phaidor's slim blade found that beloved heart? Time only would reveal the truth.

Six hundred and eighty-seven Martian days must come and go before the cell's door would again come opposite the tunnel's end where last I had seen my ever-beautiful Dejah Thoris.

Half of them had passed, or would on the morrow, yet vivid in my memory, obliterating every event that had come before or after, there remained the last scene before the gust of smoke blinded my eyes and the narrow slit that had given me sight of the interior of her cell closed between me and the Princess of Helium for a long Martian year.

As if it were yesterday, I still saw the beautiful face of Phaidor, daughter of Matai Shang, distorted with jealous rage and hatred as she sprang forward with raised dagger upon the woman I loved.

I saw the red girl, Thuvia of Ptarth, leap forward to prevent the hideous deed.

The smoke from the burning temple had come then to blot out the tragedy, but in my ears rang the single shriek as the knife fell. Then silence, and when the smoke had cleared, the revolving temple had shut off all sight or sound from the chamber in which the three beautiful women were imprisoned.

Much there had been to occupy my attention since that terrible moment; but never for an instant had the memory of the thing faded, and all the time that I could spare from the numerous duties that had devolved upon me in the reconstruction of the government of the First Born since our victorious fleet and land forces had overwhelmed them, had been spent close to the grim shaft that held the mother of my boy, Carthoris of Helium.

The race of blacks that for ages had worshiped Issus, the false deity of Mars, had been left in a state of chaos by my revealment of her as naught more than a wicked old woman. In their rage they had torn her to pieces.

From the high pinnacle of their egotism the First Born had been plunged to the depths of humiliation. Their deity was gone, and with her the whole false fabric of their religion. Their vaunted navy had fallen in defeat before the superior ships and fighting men of the red men of Helium.

Fierce green warriors from the ocher sea bottoms of outer Mars had ridden their wild thoats across the sacred gardens of the Temple of Issus, and Tars Tarkas, Jeddak of Thark, fiercest of them all, had sat upon the throne of Issus and ruled the First Born while the allies were deciding the conquered nation's fate.

Almost unanimous was the request that I ascend the ancient throne of the black men, even the First Born themselves concurring in it; but I would have none of it. My heart could never be with the race that had heaped indignities upon my princess and my son.

At my suggestion Xodar became Jeddak of the First Born. He had been a dator, or prince, until Issus had degraded him, so that his fitness for the high office bestowed was unquestioned.

The peace of the Valley Dor thus assured, the green warriors dispersed to their desolate sea bottoms, while we of Helium returned to our own country. Here again was a throne offered me, since no word had been received from the missing Jeddak of Helium, Tardos Mors, grandfather of Dejah Thoris, or his son, Mors Kajak, Jed of Helium, her father.

Over a year had elapsed since they had set out to explore the northern hemisphere in search of Carthoris, and at last their disheartened people had accepted as truth the vague rumors of their death that had filtered in from the frozen region of the pole.

Once again I refused a throne, for I would not believe that the mighty Tardos Mors, or his no less redoubtable son, was dead.

"Let one of their own blood rule you until they return," I said to the assembled nobles of Helium, as I addressed them from the Pedestal of Truth beside the Throne of Righteousness in the Temple of Reward, from the very spot where I had stood a year before when Zat Arrras pronounced the sentence of death upon me.

As I spoke I stepped forward and laid my hand upon the shoulder of Carthoris where he stood in the front rank of the circle of nobles about me.

As one, the nobles and the people lifted their voices in a long cheer of approbation. Ten thousand swords sprang on high from as many scabbards, and the glorious fighting men of ancient Helium hailed Carthoris Jeddak of Helium.

His tenure of office was to be for life or until his great-grandfather, or grandfather, should return. Having thus satisfactorily arranged this important duty for Helium, I started the following day for the Valley Dor that I might remain close to the Temple of the Sun until the fateful day that should see the opening of the prison cell where my lost love lay buried.

Hor Vastus and Kantos Kan, with my other noble lieutenants, I left with Carthoris at Helium, that he might have the benefit of their wisdom, bravery, and loyalty in the performance of the arduous duties which had devolved upon him. Only Woola, my Martian hound, accompanied me.

At my heels tonight the faithful beast moved softly in my tracks. As large as a Shetland pony, with hideous head and frightful fangs, he was indeed an awsome spectacle, as he crept after me on his ten short, muscular legs; but to me he was the embodiment of love and loyalty.

The figure ahead was that of the black dator of the First Born, Thurid, whose undying enmity I had earned that time I laid him low with my bare hands in the courtyard of the Temple of Issus, and bound him with his own harness before the noble men and women who had but a moment before been extolling his prowess.

Like many of his fellows, he had apparently accepted the

9

new order of things with good grace, and had sworn fealty to Xodar, his new ruler; but I knew that he hated me, and I was sure that in his heart he envied and hated Xodar, so I had kept a watch upon his comings and goings, to the end that of late I had become convinced that he was occupied with some manner of intrigue.

Several times I had observed him leaving the walled city of the First Born after dark, taking his way out into the cruel and horrible Valley Dor, where no honest business could lead any man.

Tonight he moved quickly along the edge of the forest until well beyond sight or sound of the city, then he turned across the crimson sward toward the shore of the Lost Sea of Korus.

The rays of the nearer moon, swinging low across the valley, touched his jewel-incrusted harness with a thousand changing lights and glanced from the glossy ebony of his smooth hide. Twice he turned his head back toward the forest, after the manner of one who is upon an evil errand, though he must have felt quite safe from pursuit.

I did not dare follow him there beneath the moonlight, since it best suited my plans not to interrupt his—I wished him to reach his destination unsuspecting, that I might learn just where that destination lay and the business that awaited the night prowler there.

So it was that I remained hidden until after Thurid had disappeared over the edge of the steep bank beside the sea a quarter of a mile away. Then, with Woola following, I hastened across the open after the black dator.

The quiet of the tomb lay upon the mysterious valley of death, crouching deep in its warm nest within the sunken area at the south pole of the dying planet. In the far distance the Golden Cliffs raised their mighty barrier faces far into the starlit heavens, the precious metals and scintillating jewels that composed them sparkling in the brilliant light of Mars's two gorgeous moons.

At my back was the forest, pruned and trimmed like the sward to parklike symmetry by the browsing of the ghoulish plant men.

Before me lay the Lost Sea of Korus, while farther on I caught the shimmering ribbon of Iss, the River of Mystery, where it wound out from beneath the Golden Cliffs to empty

10

into Korus, to which for countless ages had been borne the deluded and unhappy Martians of the outer world upon the voluntary pilgrimage to this false heaven.

The plant men, with their blood-sucking hands, and the monstrous white apes that make Dor hideous by day, were hidden in their lairs for the night.

There was no longer a Holy Thern upon the balcony in the Golden Cliffs above the Iss to summon them with weird cry to the victims floating down to their maws upon the cold, broad bosom of ancient Iss.

The navies of Helium and the First Born had cleared the fortresses and the temples of the therns when they had refused to surrender and accept the new order of things that had swept their false religion from long-suffering Mars.

In a few isolated countries they still retained their age-old power; but Matai Shang, their hekkador, Father of Therns, had been driven from his temple. Strenuous had been our endeavors to capture him; but with a few of the faithful he had escaped, and was in hiding—where we knew not.

As I came cautiously to the edge of the low cliff overlooking the Lost Sea of Korus I saw Thurid pushing out upon the bosom of the shimmering water in a small skiff—one of those strangely wrought craft of unthinkable age which the Holy Therns, with their organization of priests and lesser therns, were wont to distribute along the banks of the Iss, that the long journey of their victims might be facilitated.

Drawn up on the beach below me were a score of similar boats, each with its long pole, at one end of which was a pike, at the other a paddle. Thurid was hugging the shore, and as he passed out of sight round a near-by promontory I shoved one of the boats into the water and, calling Woola into it, pushed out from shore.

The pursuit of Thurid carried me along the edge of the sea toward the mouth of the Iss. The farther moon lay close to the horizon, casting a dense shadow beneath the cliffs that fringed the water. Thuria, the nearer moon, had set, nor would it rise again for near four hours, so that I was ensured concealing darkness for that length of time at least.

On and on went the black warrior. Now he was opposite the mouth of the Iss. Without an instant's hesitation he turned up the grim river, paddling hard against the strong current.

After him came Woola and I, closer now, for the man was

11

too intent upon forcing his craft up the river to have any eyes for what might be transpiring behind him. He hugged the shore where the current was less strong.

Presently he came to the dark cavernous portal in the face of the Golden Cliffs, through which the river poured. On into the Stygian darkness beyond he urged his craft.

It seemed hopeless to attempt to follow him here where I could not see my hand before my face, and I was almost on the point of giving up the pursuit and drifting back to the mouth of the river, there to await his return, when a sudden bend showed a faint luminosity ahead.

My quarry was plainly visible again, and in the increasing light from the phosphorescent rock that lay embedded in great patches in the roughly arched roof of the cavern I had no difficulty in following him.

It was my first trip upon the bosom of Iss, and the things I saw there will live forever in my memory.

Terrible as they were, they could not have commenced to approximate the horrible conditions which must have obtained before Tars Tarkas, the great green warrior, Xodar, the black dator, and I brought the light of truth to the outer world and stopped the mad rush of millions upon the voluntary pilgrimage to what they believed would end in a beautiful valley of peace and happiness and love.

Even now the low islands which dotted the broad stream were choked with the skeletons and half devoured carcasses of those who, through fear or a sudden awakening to the truth, had halted almost at the completion of their journey.

In the awful stench of these frightful charnel isles haggard maniacs screamed and gibbered and fought among the torn remnants of their grisly feasts; while on those which contained but clean-picked bones they battled with one another, the weaker furnishing sustenance for the stronger; or with clawlike hands clutched at the bloated bodies that drifted down with the current.

Thurid paid not the slightest attention to the screaming things that either menaced or pleaded with him as the mood directed them—evidently he was familiar with the horrid sights that surrounded him. He continued up the river for perhaps a mile; and then, crossing over to the left bank, drew his craft up on a low ledge that lay almost on a level with the water.

I dared not follow across the stream, for he most surely would have seen me. Instead I stopped close to the opposite wall beneath an overhanging mass of rock that cast a dense shadow beneath it. Here I could watch Thurid without danger of discovery.

The black was standing upon the ledge beside his boat, looking up the river, as though he were awaiting one whom he expected from that direction.

As I lay there beneath the dark rocks I noticed that a strong current seemed to flow directly toward the center of the river, so that it was difficult to hold my craft in its position. I edged farther into the shadow that I might find a hold upon the bank; but, though I proceeded several yards, I touched nothing; and then, finding that I would soon reach a point from where I could no longer see the black man, I was compelled to remain where I was, holding my position as best I could by paddling strongly against the current which flowed from beneath the rocky mass behind me.

I could not imagine what might cause this strong lateral flow, for the main channel of the river was plainly visible to me from where I sat, and I could see the rippling junction of it and the mysterious current which had aroused my curiosity.

While I was still speculating upon the phenomenon, my attention was suddenly riveted upon Thurid, who had raised both palms forward above his head in the universal salute of Martians, and a moment later his "Kaor!" the Barsoomian word of greeting, came in low but distinct tones.

I turned my eyes up the river in the direction that his were bent, and presently there came within my limited range of vision a long boat, in which were six men. Five were at the paddles, while the sixth sat in the seat of honor.

The white skins, the flowing yellow wigs which covered their bald pates, and the gorgeous diadems set in circlets of gold about their heads marked them as Holy Therns.

As they drew up beside the ledge upon which Thurid awaited them, he in the bow of the boat arose to step ashore, and then I saw that it was none other than Matai Shang, Father of Therns.

The evident cordiality with which the two men exchanged greetings filled me with wonder, for the black and white

13

men of Barsoom were hereditary enemies—nor ever before had I known of two meeting other than in battle.

Evidently the reverses that had recently overtaken both peoples had resulted in an alliance between these two individuals—at least against the common enemy—and now I saw why Thurid had come so often out into the Valley Dor by night, and that the nature of his conspiring might be such as to strike very close to me or to my friends.

I wished that I might have found a point closer to the two men from which to have heard their conversation; but it was out of the question now to attempt to cross the river, and so I lay quietly watching them, who would have given so much to have known how close I lay to them, and how easily they might have overcome and killed me with their superior force.

Several times Thurid pointed across the river in my direction, but that his gestures had any reference to me I did not for a moment believe. Presently he and Matai Shang entered the latter's boat, which turned out into the river and, swinging round, forged steadily across in my direction.

As they advanced I moved my boat farther and farther in beneath the overhanging wall, but at last it became evident that their craft was holding the same course. The five paddlers sent the larger boat ahead at a speed that taxed my energies to equal.

Every instant I expected to feel my prow crash against solid rock. The light from the river was no longer visible, but ahead I saw the faint tinge of a distant radiance, and still the water before me was open.

At last the truth dawned upon me—I was following a subterranean river which emptied into the Iss at the very point where I had hidden.

The rowers were now quite close to me. The noise of their own paddles drowned the sound of mine, but in another instant the growing light ahead would reveal me to them.

There was no time to be lost. Whatever action I was to take must be taken at once. Swinging the prow of my boat toward the right, I sought the river's rocky side, and there I lay while Matai Shang and Thurid approached up the center of the stream, which was much narrower than the Iss.

As they came nearer I heard the voices of Thurid and the Father of Therns raised in argument.

14

"I tell you, Thern," the black dator was saying, "that I wish only vengeance upon John Carter, Prince of Helium. I am leading you into no trap. What could I gain by betraying you to those who have ruined my nation and my house?"

"Let us stop here a moment that I may hear your plans," replied the hekkador, "and then we may proceed with a better understanding of our duties and obligations."

To the rowers he issued the command that brought their boat in toward the bank not a dozen paces beyond the spot where I lay.

Had they pulled in below me they must surely have seen me against the faint glow of light ahead, but from where they finally came to rest I was as secure from detection as though miles separated us.

The few words I had already overheard whetted my curiosity, and I was anxious to learn what manner of vengeance Thurid was planning against me. Nor had I long to wait. I listened intently.

"There are no obligations, Father of Therns," continued the First Born. "Thurid, Dator of Issus, has no price. When the thing has been accomplished I shall be glad if you will see to it that I am well received, as is befitting my ancient lineage and noble rank, at some court that is yet loyal to thy ancient faith, for I cannot return to the Valley Dor or elsewhere within the power of the Prince of Helium; but even that I do not demand—it shall be as your own desire in the matter directs."

"It shall be as you wish, Dator," replied Matai Shang; "nor is that all—power and riches shall be yours if you restore my daughter, Phaidor, to me, and place within my power Dejah Thoris, Princess of Helium.

"Ah," he continued with a malicious snarl, "but the Earth man shall suffer for the indignities he has put upon the holy of holies, nor shall any vileness be too vile to inflict upon his princess. Would that it were in my power to force him to witness the humiliation and degradation of the red woman."

"You shall have your way with her before another day has passed, Matai Shang," said Thurid, "if you but say the word."

"I have heard of the Temple of the Sun, Dator," replied Matai Shang, "but never have I heard that its prisoners could be released before the allotted year of their incarceration had elapsed. How, then, may you accomplish the impossible?"

"Access may be had to any cell of the temple at any time," replied Thurid. "Only Issus knew this; nor was it ever Issus' way to divulge more of her secrets than were necessary. By chance, after her death, I came upon an ancient plan of the temple, and there I found, plainly writ, the most minute directions for reaching the cells at any time.

"And more I learned—that many men had gone thither for Issus in the past, always on errands of death and torture to the prisoners; but those who thus learned the secret way were wont to die mysteriously immediately they had returned and made their reports to cruel Issus."

"Let us proceed, then," said Matai Shang at last. "I must trust you, yet at the same time you must trust me, for we are six to your one."

"I do not fear," replied Thurid, "nor need you. Our hatred of the common enemy is sufficient bond to insure our loyalty to each other, and after we have defiled the Princess of Helium there will be still greater reason for the maintenance of our allegiance—unless I greatly mistake the temper of her lord."

Matai Shang spoke to the paddlers. The boat moved on up the tributary.

It was with difficulty that I restrained myself from rushing upon them and slaying the two vile plotters; but quickly I saw the mad rashness of such an act, which would cut down the only man who could lead the way to Dejah Thoris' prison before the long Martian year had swung its interminable circle.

If he should lead Matai Shang to that hollowed spot, then, too, should he lead John Carter, Prince of Helium.

With silent paddle I swung slowly into the wake of the larger craft.

UNDER THE MOUNTAINS

As WE advanced up the river which winds beneath the Golden Cliffs out of the bowels of the Mountains of Otz to mingle its dark waters with the grim and mysterious Iss the faint glow which had appeared before us grew gradually into an all-enveloping radiance.

The river widened until it presented the aspect of a large lake whose vaulted dome, lighted by glowing phosphorescent rock, was splashed with the vivid rays of the diamond, the sapphire, the ruby, and the countless, nameless jewels of Barsoom which lay incrusted in the virgin gold which forms the major portion of these magnificent cliffs.

Beyond the lighted chamber of the lake was darkness—what lay behind the darkness I could not even guess.

To have followed the thern boat across the gleaming water would have been to invite instant detection, and so, though I was loath to permit Thurid to pass even for an instant beyond my sight, I was forced to wait in the shadows until the other boat had passed from my sight at the far extremity of the lake.

Then I paddled out upon the brilliant surface in the direction they had taken.

When, after what seemed an eternity, I reached the shadows at the upper end of the lake I found that the river issued from a low aperture, to pass beneath which it was necessary that I compel Woola to lie flat in the boat, and I, myself, must need bend double before the low roof cleared my head.

Immediately the roof rose again upon the other side, but no longer was the way brilliantly lighted. Instead only a feeble glow emanated from small and scattered patches of phosphorescent rock in wall and roof.

Directly before me the river ran into this smaller chamber through three separate arched openings.

Thurid and the therns were nowhere to be seen—into which of the dark holes had they disappeared? There was no means by which I might know, and so I chose the center opening as being as likely to lead me in the right direction as another.

Here the way was through utter darkness. The stream was narrow—so narrow that in the blackness I was constantly bumping first one rock wall and then another as the river wound hither and thither along its flinty bed.

Far ahead I presently heard a deep and sullen roar which increased in volume as I advanced, and then broke upon my ears with all the intensity of its mad fury as I swung round a sharp curve into a dimly lighted stretch of water.

Directly before me the river thundered down from above in a mighty waterfall that filled the narrow gorge from side to side, rising far above me several hundred feet—as magnificent a spectacle as I ever had seen.

But the roar—the awful, deafening roar of those tumbling waters penned in the rocky, subterranean vault! Had the fall not entirely blocked my further passage and shown me that I had followed the wrong course I believe that I should have fled anyway before the maddening tumult.

Thurid and the therns could not have come this way. By stumbling upon the wrong course I had lost the trail, and they had gained so much ahead of me that now I might not be able to find them before it was too late, if, in fact, I could find them at all.

It had taken several hours to force my way up to the falls against the strong current, and other hours would be required for the descent, although the pace would be much swifter.

With a sigh I turned the prow of my craft down stream, and with mighty strokes hastened with reckless speed through the dark and tortuous channel until once again I came to the chamber into which flowed the three branches of the river.

Two unexplored channels still remained from which to choose; nor was there any means by which I could judge which was the more likely to lead me to the plotters.

Never in my life, that I can recall, have I suffered such an agony of indecision. So much depended upon a correct choice; so much depended upon haste.

The hours that I had already lost might seal the fate of the incomparable Dejah Thoris were she not already dead—to sacrifice other hours, and maybe days in a fruitless exploration of another blind lead would unquestionably prove fatal.

Several times I essayed the right-hand entrance only to turn back as though warned by some strange intuitive sense that this was not the way. At last, convinced by the oft-recurring phenomenon, I cast my all upon the left-hand archway; yet it was with a lingering doubt that I turned a parting look at the sullen waters which rolled, dark and forbidding, from beneath the grim, low archway on the right.

And as I looked there came bobbing out upon the current from the Stygian darkness of the interior the shell of one of the great, succulent fruits of the sorapus tree.

I could scarce restrain a shout of elation as this silent, insensate messenger floated past me, on toward the Iss and Korus, for it told me that journeying Martians were above me on that very stream.

They had eaten of this marvelous fruit which nature concentrates within the hard shell of the sorapus nut, and having eaten had cast the husk overboard. It could have come from no others than the party I sought.

Quickly I abandoned all thought of the left-hand passage, and a moment later had turned into the right. The stream soon widened, and recurring areas of phosphorescent rock lighted my way.

I made good time, but was convinced that I was nearly a day behind those I was tracking. Neither Woola nor I had eaten since the previous day, but in so far as he was concerned it mattered but little, since practically all the animals of the dead sea bottoms of Mars are able to go for incredible periods without nourishment.

Nor did I suffer. The water of the river was sweet and cold, for it was unpolluted by decaying bodies—unlike the Iss —and as for food, why the mere thought that I was nearing my beloved princess raised me above every material want.

As I proceeded, the river became narrower and the current swift and turbulent—so swift in fact that it was with difficulty that I forced my craft upward at all. I could not have been making to exceed a hundred yards an hour when, at a bend, I was confronted by a series of rapids through which the river foamed and boiled at a terrific rate.

My heart sank within me. The sorapus nutshell had proved a false prophet, and, after all, my intuition had been correct —it was the left-hand channel that I should have followed.

Had I been a woman I should have wept. At my right was a great, slow-moving eddy that circled far beneath the cliff's overhanging side, and to rest my tired muscles before turning back I let my boat drift into its embrace.

I was almost prostrated by disappointment. It would mean another half-day's loss of time to retrace my way and take the only passage that yet remained unexplored. What hellish fate had led me to select from three possible avenues the two that were wrong?

As the lazy current of the eddy carried me slowly about the periphery of the watery circle my boat twice touched the rocky side of the river in the dark recess beneath the cliff. A third time it struck, gently as it had before, but the contact resulted in a different sound—the sound of wood scraping upon wood.

In an instant I was on the alert, for there could be no wood within that buried river that had not been man brought. Almost coincidentally with my first apprehension of the noise, my hand shot out across the boat's side, and a second later I felt my fingers gripping the gunwale of another craft.

As though turned to stone I sat in tense and rigid silence, straining my eyes into the utter darkness before me in an effort to discover if the boat were occupied.

It was entirely possible that there might be men on board it who were still ignorant of my presence, for the boat was scraping gently against the rocks upon one side, so that the gentle touch of my boat upon the other easily could have gone unnoticed.

Peer as I would I could not penetrate the darkness, and then I listened intently for the sound of breathing near me; but except for the noise of the rapids, the soft scraping of the boats, and the lapping of the water at their sides I could distinguish no sound. As usual, I thought rapidly.

A rope lay coiled in the bottom of my own craft. Very softly I gathered it up, and making one end fast to the bronze ring in the prow I stepped gingerly into the boat beside me. In one hand I grasped the rope, in the other my keen long-sword.

For a full minute, perhaps, I stood motionless after entering the strange craft. It had rocked a trifle beneath my weight, but it had been the scraping of its side against the side of my own boat that had seemed most likely to alarm its occupants, if there were any.

But there was no answering sound, and a moment later I had felt from stem to stern and found the boat deserted.

Groping with my hands along the face of the rocks to which the craft was moored, I discovered a narrow ledge which I knew must be the avenue taken by those who had come before me. That they could be none other than Thurid and his party I was convinced by the size and build of the boat I had found.

Calling to Woola to follow me I stepped out upon the ledge. The great, savage brute, agile as a cat, crept after me.

As he passed through the boat that had been occupied by Thurid and the therns he emitted a single low growl, and when he came beside me upon the ledge and my hand rested upon his neck I felt his short mane bristling with anger. I think he sensed telepathically the recent presence of an enemy, for I had made no effort to impart to him the nature of our quest or the status of those we tracked.

This omission I now made haste to correct, and, after the manner of green Martians with their beasts, I let him know partially by the weird and uncanny telepathy of Barsoom and partly by word of mouth that we were upon the trail of those who had recently occupied the boat through which we had just passed.

A soft purr, like that of a great cat, indicated that Woola understood, and then, with a word to him to follow, I turned to the right along the ledge, but scarcely had I done so than I felt his mighty fangs tugging at my leathern harness.

As I turned to discover the cause of his act he continued to pull me steadily in the opposite direction, nor would he desist until I had turned about and indicated that I would follow him voluntarily.

Never had I known him to be in error in a matter of tracking, so it was with a feeling of entire security that I moved cautiously in the huge beast's wake. Through Cimmerian darkness he moved along the narrow ledge beside the boiling rapids.

As we advanced, the way led from beneath the overhanging cliffs out into a dim light, and then it was that I saw that the trail had been cut from the living rock, and that it ran up along the river's side beyond the rapids.

For hours we followed the dark and gloomy river farther and farther into the bowels of Mars. From the direction and

21

distance I knew that we must be well beneath the Valley Dor, and possibly beneath the Sea of Omean as well—it could not be much farther now to the Temple of the Sun.

Even as my mind framed the thought Woola halted suddenly before a narrow, arched doorway in the cliff by the trail's side. Quickly he crouched back away from the entrance, at the same time turning his eyes toward me.

Words could not have more plainly told me that danger of some sort lay near by, and so I pressed quietly forward to his side, and passing him looked into the aperture at our right.

Before me was a fair-sized chamber that, from its appointments, I knew must have at one time been a guardroom. There were racks for weapons, and slightly raised platforms for the sleeping silks and furs of the warriors, but now its only occupants were two of the therns who had been of the party with Thurid and Matai Shang.

The men were in earnest conversation, and from their tones it was apparent that they were entirely unaware that they had listeners.

"I tell you," one of them was saying, "I do not trust the black one. There was no necessity for leaving us here to guard the way. Against what, pray, should we guard this long-forgotten, abysmal path? It was but a ruse to divide our numbers.

"He will have Matai Shang leave others elsewhere on some pretext or other, and then at last he will fall upon us with his confederates and slay us all."

"I believe you, Lakor," replied the other, "there can never be aught else than deadly hatred between thern and First Born. And what think you of the ridiculous matter of the light? 'Let the light shine with the intensity of three radium units for fifty tals, and for one xat let it shine with the intensity of one radium unit, and then for twenty-five tals with nine units.' Those were his very words, and to think that wise old Matai Shang should listen to such foolishness."

"Indeed, it is silly," replied Lakor. "It will open nothing other than the way to a quick death for us all. He had to make some answer when Matai Shang asked him flatly what he should do when he came to the Temple of the Sun, and so he made his answer quickly from his imagination—I would wager a hekkador's diadem that he could not now repeat it himself."

"Let us not remain here longer, Lakor," spoke the other thern. "Perchance if we hasten after them we may come in time to rescue Matai Shang, and wreak our own vengeance upon the black dator. What say you?"

"Never in a long life," answered Lakor, "have I disobeyed a single command of the Father of Therns. I shall stay here until I rot if he does not return to bid me elsewhere."

Lakor's companion shook his head.

"You are my superior," he said; "I cannot do other than you sanction, though I still believe that we are foolish to remain."

I, too, thought that they were foolish to remain, for I saw from Woola's actions that the trail led through the room where the two therns held guard. I had no reason to harbor any considerable love for this race of self-deified demons, yet I would have passed them by were it possible without molesting them.

It was worth trying anyway, for a fight might delay us considerably, or even put an end entirely to my search—better men than I have gone down before fighters of meaner ability than that possessed by the fierce thern warriors.

Signaling Woola to heel I stepped suddenly into the room before the two men. At sight of me their long-swords flashed from the harness at their sides, but I raised my hand in a gesture of restraint.

"I seek Thurid, the black dator," I said. "My quarrel is with him, not with you. Let me pass then in peace, for if I mistake not he is as much your enemy as mine, and you can have no cause to protect him."

They lowered their swords and Lakor spoke.

"I know not whom you may be, with the white skin of a thern and the black hair of a red man; but were it only Thurid whose safety were at stake you might pass, and welcome, in so far as we be concerned.

"Tell us who you be, and what mission calls you to this unknown world beneath the Valley Dor, then maybe we can see our way to let you pass upon the errand which we should like to undertake would our orders permit."

I was surprised that neither of them had recognized me, for I thought that I was quite sufficiently well known either by personal experience or reputation to every thern upon Barsoom as to make my identity immediately apparent in any part of the planet. In fact, I was the only white man upon Mars whose hair was black and whose eyes were gray, with the exception of my son, Carthoris.

To reveal my identity might be to precipitate an attack, for every thern upon Barsoom knew that to me they owed the fall of their age-old spiritual supremacy. On the other hand my reputation as a fighting man might be sufficient to pass me by these two were their livers not of the right complexion to welcome a battle to the death.

To be quite candid I did not attempt to delude myself with any such sophistry, since I knew well that upon warlike Mars there are few cowards, and that every man, whether prince, priest, or peasant, glories in deadly strife. And so I gripped my long-sword the tighter as I replied to Lakor.

"I believe that you will see the wisdom of permitting me to pass unmolested," I said, "for it would avail you nothing to die uselessly in the rocky bowels of Barsoom merely to protect a hereditary enemy, such as Thurid, Dator of the First Born.

"That you shall die should you elect to oppose me is evidenced by the moldering corpses of all the many great Barsoomian warriors who have gone down beneath this blade—I am John Carter, Prince of Helium."

For a moment that name seemed to paralyze the two men; but only for a moment, and then the younger of them, with a vile name upon his lips, rushed toward me with ready sword.

He had been standing a little behind his companion, Lakor, during our parley, and now, ere he could engage me, the older man grasped his harness and drew him back.

"Hold!" commanded Lakor. "There will be plenty of time to fight if we find it wise to fight at all. There be good reasons why every thern upon Barsoom should yearn to spill the blood of the blasphemer, the sacrilegist; but let us mix wisdom with our righteous hate. The Prince of Helium is bound upon an errand which we ourselves, but a moment since, were wishing that we might undertake.

"Let him go then and slay the black. When he returns we shall still be here to bar his way to the outer world, and thus we shall have rid ourselves of two enemies, nor have incurred the displeasure of the Father of Therns."

24

As he spoke I could not but note the crafty glint in his evil eyes, and while I saw the apparent logic of his reasoning I felt, subconsciously perhaps, that his words did but veil some sinister intent. The other thern turned toward him in evident surprise, but when Lakor had whispered a few brief words into his ear he, too, drew back and nodded acquiescence to his superior's suggestion.

"Proceed, John Carter," said Lakor; "but know that if Thurid does not lay you low there will be those awaiting your return who will see that you never pass again into the sunlight of the upper world. Go!"

During our conversation Woola had been growling and bristling close to my side. Occasionally he would look up into my face with a low, pleading whine, as though begging for the word that would send him headlong at the bare throats before him. He, too, sensed the villainy behind the smooth words.

Beyond the therns several doorways opened off the guardroom, and toward the one upon the extreme right Lakor motioned.

"That way leads to Thurid," he said.

But when I would have called Woola to follow me there the beast whined and held back, and at last ran quickly to the first opening at the left, where he stood emitting his coughing bark, as though urging me to follow him upon the right way.

I turned a questioning look upon Lakor.

"The brute is seldom wrong," I said, "and while I do not doubt your superior knowledge, Thern, I think that I shall do well to listen to the voice of instinct that is backed by love and loyalty."

As I spoke I smiled grimly that he might know without words that I distrusted him.

"As you will," the fellow replied with a shrug. "In the end it shall be all the same."

I turned and followed Woola into the left-hand passage, and though my back was toward my enemies, my ears were on the alert; yet I heard no sound of pursuit. The passageway was dimly lighted by occasional radium bulbs, the universal lighting medium of Barsoom.

These same lamps may have been doing continuous duty in these subterranean chambers for ages, since they require no

25

attention and are so compounded that they give off but the minutest of their substance in the generation of years of luminosity.

We had proceeded for but a short distance when we commenced to pass the mouths of diverging corridors, but not once did Woola hesitate. It was at the opening to one of these corridors upon my right that I presently heard a sound that spoke more plainly to John Carter, fighting man, than could the words of my mother tongue—it was the clank of metal—the metal of a warrior's harness—and it came from a little distance up the corridor upon my right.

Woola heard it, too, and like a flash he had wheeled and stood facing the threatened danger, his mane all abristle and all his rows of glistening fangs bared by snarling, backdrawn lips. With a gesture I silenced him, and together we drew aside into another corridor a few paces farther on.

Here we waited; nor did we have long to wait, for presently we saw the shadows of two men fall upon the floor of the main corridor athwart the doorway of our hiding place. Very cautiously they were moving now—the accidental clank that had alarmed me was not repeated.

Presently they came opposite our station; nor was I surprised to see that the two were Lakor and his companion of the guardroom.

They walked very softly, and in the right hand of each gleamed a keen long-sword. They halted quite close to the entrance of our retreat, whispering to each other.

"Can it be that we have distanced them already?" said Lakor.

"Either that or the beast has led the man upon a wrong trail," replied the other, "for the way which we took is by far the shorter to this point—for him who knows it. John Carter would have found it a short road to death had he taken it as you suggested to him."

"Yes," said Lakor, "no amount of fighting ability would have saved him from the pivoted flagstone. He surely would have stepped upon it, and by now, if the pit beneath it has a bottom, which Thurid denies, he should have been rapidly approaching it. Curses on that calot of his that warned him toward the safer avenue!"

"There be other dangers ahead of him, though," spoke Lakor's fellow, "which he may not so easily escape—should

26

he succeed in escaping our two good swords. Consider, for example, what chance he will have, coming unexpectedly into the chamber of——"

I would have given much to have heard the balance of that conversation that I might have been warned of the perils that lay ahead, but fate intervened, and just at the very instant of all other instants that I would not have elected to do it, I sneezed.

THE TEMPLE OF THE SUN

THERE was nothing for it now other than to fight; nor did I have any advantage as I sprang, sword in hand, into the corridor before the two therns, for my untimely sneeze had warned them of my presence and they were ready for me.

There were no words, for they would have been a waste of breath. The very presence of the two proclaimed their treachery. That they were following to fall upon me unawares was all too plain, and they, of course, must have known that I understood their plan.

In an instant I was engaged with both, and though I loathe the very name of thern, I must in all fairness admit that they are mighty swordsmen; and these two were no exception, unless it were that they were even more skilled and fearless than the average among their race.

While it lasted it was indeed as joyous a conflict as I ever had experienced. Twice at least I saved my breast from the mortal thrust of piercing steel only by the wondrous agility with which my earthly muscles endow me under the conditions of lesser gravity and air pressure upon Mars.

Yet even so I came near to tasting death that day in the gloomy corridor beneath Mars's southern pole, for Lakor played a trick upon me that in all my experience of fighting upon two planets I never before had witnessed the like of.

The other thern was engaging me at the time, and I was forcing him back—touching him here and there with my point until he was bleeding from a dozen wounds, yet not being able to penetrate his marvelous guard to reach a vulnerable spot for the brief instant that would have been sufficient to send him to his ancestors.

It was then that Lakor quickly unslung a belt from his harness, and as I stepped back to parry a wicked thrust he lashed one end of it about my left ankle so that it wound there for an instant, while he jerked suddenly upon the other end, throwing me heavily upon my back.

Then, like leaping panthers, they were upon me; but they

28

had reckoned without Woola, and before ever a blade touched me, a roaring embodiment of a thousand demons hurtled above my prostrate form and my loyal Martian calot was upon them.

Imagine, if you can, a huge grizzly with ten legs armed with mighty talons and an enormous froglike mouth splitting his head from ear to ear, exposing three rows of long, white tusks. Then endow this creature of your imagination with the agility and ferocity of a half-starved Bengal tiger and the strength of a span of bulls, and you will have some faint conception of Woola in action.

Before I could call him off he had crushed Lakor into a jelly with a single blow of one mighty paw, and had literally torn the other thern to ribbons; yet when I spoke to him sharply he cowed sheepishly as though he had done a thing to deserve censure and chastisement.

Never had I had the heart to punish Woola during the long years that had passed since that first day upon Mars when the green jed of the Tharks had placed him on guard over me, and I had won his love and loyalty from the cruel and loveless masters of his former life, yet I believe he would have submitted to any cruelty that I might have inflicted upon him, so wondrous was his affection for me.

The diadem in the center of the circlet of gold upon the brow of Lakor proclaimed him a Holy Thern, while his companion, not thus adorned, was a lesser thern, though from his harness I gleaned that he had reached the Ninth Cycle, which is but one below that of the Holy Therns.

As I stood for a moment looking at the gruesome havoc Woola had wrought, there recurred to me the memory of that other occasion upon which I had masqueraded in the wig, diadem, and harness of Sator Throg, the Holy Thern whom Thuvia of Ptarth had slain, and now it occurred to me that it might prove of worth to utilize Lakor's trappings for the same purpose.

A moment later I had torn his yellow wig from his bald pate and transferred it and the circlet, as well as all his harness, to my own person.

Woola did not approve of the metamorphosis. He sniffed at me and growled ominously, but when I spoke to him and patted his huge head he at length became reconciled to the change, and at my command trotted off along the corridor in the direction we had been going when our progress had been interrupted by the therns.

We moved cautiously now, warned by the fragment of conversation I had overheard. I kept abreast of Woola that we might have the benefit of all our eyes for what might appear suddenly ahead to menace us, and well it was that we were forewarned.

At the bottom of a flight of narrow steps the corridor turned sharply back upon itself, immediately making another turn in the original direction, so that at that point it formed a perfect letter S, the top leg of which debouched suddenly into a large chamber, illy lighted, and the floor of which was completely covered by venomous snakes and loathsome reptiles.

To have attempted to cross that floor would have been to court instant death, and for a moment I was almost completely discouraged. Then it occurred to me that Thurid and Matai Shang with their party must have crossed it, and so there was a way.

Had it not been for the fortunate accident by which I overheard even so small a portion of the therns' conversation we should have blundered at least a step or two into that wriggling mass of destruction, and a single step would have been all-sufficient to have sealed our doom.

These were the only reptiles I had ever seen upon Barsoom, but I knew from their similarity to the fossilized remains of supposedly extinct species I had seen in the museums of Helium that they comprised many of the known prehistoric reptilian genera, as well as others undiscovered.

A more hideous aggregation of monsters had never before assailed my vision. It would be futile to attempt to describe them to Earth men, since substance is the only thing which they possess in common with any creature of the past or present with which you are familiar—even their venom is of an unearthly virulence that, by comparison, would make the cobra de capello seem quite as harmless as an angleworm.

As they spied me there was a concerted rush by those nearest the entrance where we stood, but a line of radium bulbs inset along the threshold of their chamber brought them to a sudden halt—evidently they dared not cross that line of light.

I had been quite sure that they would not venture beyond the room in which I had discovered them, though I had not guessed at what deterred them. The simple fact that we had found no reptiles in the corridor through which we had just come was sufficient assurance that they did not venture there.

I drew Woola out of harm's way, and then began a careful survey of as much of the Chamber of Reptiles as I could see from where I stood. As my eyes became accustomed to the dim light of its interior I gradually made out a low gallery at the far end of the apartment from which opened several exits.

Coming as close to the threshold as I dared, I followed this gallery with my eyes, discovering that it circled the room as far as I could see. Then I glanced above me along the upper edge of the entrance to which we had come, and there, to my delight, I saw an end of the gallery not a foot above my head. In an instant I had leaped to it and called Woola after me.

Here there were no reptiles—the way was clear to the opposite side of the hideous chamber—and a moment later Woola and I dropped down to safety in the corridor beyond.

Not ten minutes later we came into a vast circular apartment of white marble, the walls of which were inlaid with gold in the strange hieroglyphics of the First Born.

From the high dome of this mighty apartment a huge circular column extended to the floor, and as I watched I saw that it slowly revolved.

I had reached the base of the Temple of the Sun!

Somewhere above me lay Dejah Thoris, and with her were Phaidor, daughter of Matai Shang, and Thuvia of Ptarth. But how to reach them, now that I had found the only vulnerable spot in their mighty prison, was still a baffling riddle.

Slowly I circled the great shaft, looking for a means of ingress. Part way around I found a tiny radium flash torch, and as I examined it in mild curiosity as to its presence there in this almost inaccessible and unknown spot, I came suddenly upon the insignia of the house of Thurid jewel-inset in its metal case.

I am upon the right trail, I thought, as I slipped the bauble into the pocket-pouch which hung from my harness.

31

Then I continued my search for the entrance, which I knew must be somewhere about; nor had I long to search, for almost immediately thereafter I came upon a small door so cunningly inlaid in the shaft's base that it might have passed unnoticed by a less keen or careful observer.

There was the door that would lead me within the prison, but where was the means to open it? No button or lock were visible. Again and again I went carefully over every square inch of its surface, but the most that I could find was a tiny pinhole a little above and to the right of the door's center—a pinhole that seemed only an accident of manufacture or an imperfection of material.

Into this minute aperture I attempted to peer, but whether it was but a fraction of an inch deep or passed completely through the door I could not tell—at least no light showed beyond it. I put my ear to it next and listened, but again my efforts brought negligible results.

During these experiments Woola had been standing at my side gazing intently at the door, and as my glance fell upon him it occurred to me to test the correctness of my hypothesis, that this portal had been the means of ingress to the temple used by Thurid, the black dator, and Matai Shang, Father of Therns.

Turning away abruptly, I called to him to follow me. For a moment he hesitated, and then leaped after me, whining and tugging at my harness to draw me back. I walked on, however, some distance from the door before I let him have his way, that I might see precisely what he would do. Then I permitted him to lead me wherever he would.

Straight back to that baffling portal he dragged me, again taking up his position facing the blank stone, gazing straight at its shining surface. For an hour I worked to solve the mystery of the combination that would open the way before me.

Carefully I recalled every circumstance of my pursuit of Thurid, and my conclusion was identical with my original belief—that Thurid had come this way without other assistance than his own knowledge and passed through the door that barred my progress, unaided from within. But how had he accomplished it?

I recalled the incident of the Chamber of Mystery in the Golden Cliffs that time I had freed Thuvia of Ptarth from the dungeon of the therns, and she had taken a slender, needle-like key from the keyring of her dead jailer to open the door leading back into the Chamber of Mystery where Tars Tarkas fought for his life with the great banths. Such a tiny keyhole as now defied me had opened the way to the intricate lock in that other door.

Hastily I dumped the contents of my pocket-pouch upon the ground before me. Could I but find a slender bit of steel I might yet fashion a key that would give me ingress to the temple prison.

As I examined the heterogeneous collection of odds and ends that is always to be found in the pocket-pouch of a Martian warrior my hand fell upon the emblazoned radium flash torch of the black dator.

As I was about to lay the thing aside as of no value in my present predicament my eyes chanced upon a few strange characters roughly and freshly scratched upon the soft gold of the case.

Casual curiosity prompted me to decipher them, but what I read carried no immediate meaning to my mind. There were three sets of characters, one below another:

$$3 \mid\!-\!\mid 50 \text{ T}$$
$$1 \mid\!-\!\mid 1 \text{ X}$$
$$9 \mid\!-\!\mid 25 \text{ T}$$

For only an instant my curiosity was piqued, and then I replaced the torch in my pocket-pouch, but my fingers had not unclasped from it when there rushed to my memory the recollection of the conversation between Lakor and his companion when the lesser thern had quoted the words of Thurid and scoffed at them: "And what think you of the ridiculous matter of the light? Let the light shine with the intensity of three radium units for fifty tals"—ah, there was the first line of characters upon the torch's metal case—3— 50 T; "and for one xat let it shine with the intensity of one radium unit"—there was the second line; "and then for twenty-five tals with nine units."

The formula was complete; but—what did it mean?

I thought I knew, and, seizing a powerful magnifying glass from the litter of my pocket-pouch, I applied myself to a careful examination of the marble immediately about the pinhole in the door. I could have cried aloud in exultation when my scrutiny disclosed the almost invisible incrustation of particles of carbonized electrons which are thrown off by these Martian torches.

It was evident that for countless ages radium torches had been applied to this pinhole, and for what purpose there could be but a single answer—the mechanism of the lock was actuated by light rays; and I, John Carter, Prince of Helium, held the combination in my hand—scratched by the hand of my enemy upon his own torch case.

In a cylindrical bracelet of gold about my wrist was my Barsoomian chronometer—a delicate instrument that records the tals and xats and zodes of `Martian time, presenting them to view beneath a strong crystal much after the manner of an earthly odometer.

Timing my operations carefully, I held the torch to the small aperture in the door, regulating the intensity of the light by means of the thumb-lever upon the side of the case.

For fifty tals I let three units of light shine full in the pinhole, then one unit for one xat, and for twenty-five tals nine units. Those last twenty-five tals were the longest twenty-five seconds of my life. Would the lock click at the end of those seemingly interminable intervals of time?

Twenty-three! Twenty-four! Twenty-five!

I shut off the light with a snap. For seven tals I waited—there had been no appreciable effect upon the lock's mechanism. Could it be that my theory was entirely wrong?

Hold! Had the nervous strain resulted in a hallucination, or did the door really move? Slowly the solid stone sank noiselessly back into the wall—there was no hallucination here.

Back and back it slid for ten feet until it had disclosed at its right a narrow doorway leading into a dark and narrow corridor that paralleled the outer wall. Scarcely was the entrance uncovered than Woola and I had leaped through —then the door slipped quietly back into place.

Down the corridor at some distance I saw the faint reflection of a light, and toward this we made our way. At the point where the light shone was a sharp turn, and a little distance beyond this a brilliantly lighted chamber.

Here we discovered a spiral stairway leading up from the center of the circular room.

Immediately I knew that we had reached the center of the base of the Temple of the Sun—the spiral runway led upward past the inner walls of the prison cells. Somewhere above me was Dejah Thoris, unless Thurid and Matai Shang had already succeeded in stealing her.

We had scarcely started up the runway when Woola suddenly displayed the wildest excitement. He leaped back and forth, snapping at my legs and harness, until I thought that he was mad, and finally when I pushed him from me and started once more to ascend he grasped my sword arm between his jaws and dragged me back.

No amount of scolding or cuffing would suffice to make him release me, and I was entirely at the mercy of his brute strength unless I cared to use my dagger upon him with my left hand; but, mad or no, I had not the heart to run the sharp blade into that faithful body.

Down into the chamber he dragged me, and across it to the side opposite that at which we had entered. Here was another doorway leading into a corridor which ran directly down a steep incline. Without a moment's hesitation Woola jerked me along this rocky passage.

Presently he stopped and released me, standing between me and the way we had come, looking up into my face as though to ask if I would now follow him voluntarily or if he must still resort to force.

Looking ruefully at the marks of his great teeth upon my bare arm I decided to do as he seemed to wish me to do. After all, his strange instinct might be more dependable than my faulty human judgment.

And well it was that I had been forced to follow him. But a short distance from the circular chamber we came suddenly into a brilliantly lighted labyrinth of crystal glass partitioned passages.

At first I thought it was one vast, unbroken chamber, so clear and transparent were the walls of the winding corridors, but after I had nearly brained myself a couple of times by attempting to pass through solid vitreous walls I went more carefully.

We had proceeded but a few yards along the corridor that had given us entrance to this strange maze when Woola gave mouth to a most frightful roar, at the same time dashing against the clear partition at our left.

The resounding echoes of that fearsome cry were still reverberating through the subterranean chambers when I saw the thing that had startled it from the faithful beast.

Far in the distance, dimly through the many thicknesses of intervening crystal, as in a haze that made them seem unreal and ghostly, I discerned the figures of eight people—three females and five men.

At the same instant, evidently startled by Woola's fierce cry, they halted and looked about. Then, of a sudden, one of them, a woman, held her arms out toward me, and even at that great distance I could see that her lips moved—it was Dejah Thoris, my ever beautiful and ever youthful Princess of Helium.

With her were Thuvia of Ptarth, Phaidor, daughter of Matai Shang, and Thurid, and the Father of Therns, and the three lesser therns that had accompanied them.

Thurid shook his fist at me, and then two of the therns grasped Dejah Thoris and Thuvia roughly by their arms and hurried them on. A moment later they had disappeared into a stone corridor beyond the labyrinth of glass.

They say that love is blind; but so great a love as that of Dejah Thoris that knew me even beneath the thern disguise I wore and across the misty vista of that crystal maze must indeed be far from blind.

THE SECRET TOWER

I HAVE no stomach to narrate the monotonous events of the tedious days that Woola and I spent ferreting our way across the labyrinth of glass, through the dark and devious ways beyond that led beneath the Valley Dor and Golden Cliffs to emerge at last upon the flank of the Otz Mountains just above the Valley of Lost Souls—that pitiful purgatory peopled by the poor unfortunates who dare not continue their abandoned pilgrimage to Dor, or return to the various lands of the outer world from whence they came.

Here the trail of Dejah Thoris' abductors led along the mountains' base, across steep and rugged ravines, by the side of appalling precipices, and sometimes out into the valley, where we found fighting aplenty with the members of the various tribes that make up the population of this vale of hopelessness.

But through it all we came at last to where the way led up a narrow gorge that grew steeper and more impracticable at every step until before us loomed a mighty fortress buried beneath the side of an overhanging cliff.

Here was the secret hiding place of Matai Shang, Father of Therns. Here, surrounded by a handful of the faithful, the hekkador of the ancient faith, who had once been served by millions of vassals and dependents, dispensed the spiritual word among the half dozen nations of Barsoom that still clung tenaciously to their false and discredited religion.

Darkness was just falling as we came in sight of the seemingly impregnable walls of this mountain stronghold, and lest we be seen I drew back with Woola behind a jutting granite promontory, into a clump of the hardy, purple scrub that thrives upon the barren sides of Otz.

Here we lay until the quick transition from daylight to darkness had passed. Then I crept out to approach the fortress walls in search of a way within.

Either through carelessness or over-confidence in the supposed inaccessibility of their hiding place, the triple-barred gate stood ajar. Beyond were a handful of guards, laughing and talking over one of their incomprehensible Barsoomian games.

I saw that none of the guardsmen had been of the party that accompanied Thurid and Matai Shang; and so, relying entirely upon my disguise, I walked boldly through the gateway and up to the thern guard.

The men stopped their game and looked up at me, but there was no sign of suspicion. Similarly they looked at Woola, growling at my heel.

"Kaor!" I said in true Martian greeting, and the warriors arose and saluted me. "I have but just found my way hither from the Golden Cliffs," I continued, "and seek audience with the hekkador, Matai Shang, Father of Therns. Where may he be found?"

"Follow me," said one of the guard, and, turning, led me across the outer courtyard toward a second buttressed wall.

Why the apparent ease with which I seemingly deceived them did not rouse my suspicions I know not, unless it was that my mind was still so full of that fleeting glimpse of my beloved princess that there was room in it for naught else. Be that as it may, the fact is that I marched buoyantly behind my guide straight into the jaws of death.

Afterward I learned that thern spies had been aware of my coming for hours before I reached the hidden fortress.

The gate had been purposely left ajar to tempt me on. The guards had been schooled well in their part of the conspiracy; and I, more like a schoolboy than a seasoned warrior, ran headlong into the trap.

At the far side of the outer court a narrow door let into the angle made by one of the buttresses with the wall. Here my guide produced a key and opened the way within; then, stepping back, he motioned me to enter.

"Matai Shang is in the temple court beyond," he said; and as Woola and I passed through, the fellow closed the door quickly upon us.

The nasty laugh that came to my ears through the heavy planking of the door after the lock clicked was my first intimation that all was not as it should be.

I found myself in a small, circular chamber within the buttress. Before me a door opened, presumably, upon the inner court beyond. For a moment I hesitated, all my suspicions now suddenly, though tardily, aroused; then, with a shrug of my shoulders, I opened the door and stepped out into the glare of torches that lighted the inner court.

Directly opposite me a massive tower rose to a height of three hundred feet. It was of the strangely beautiful modern Barsoomian style of architecture, its entire surface hand carved in bold relief with intricate and fanciful designs. Thirty feet above the courtyard and overlooking it was a broad balcony, and there, indeed, was Matai Shang, and with him were Thurid and Phaidor, Thuvia, and Dejah Thoris—the last two heavily ironed. A handful of thern warriors stood just behind the little party.

As I entered the enclosure the eyes of those in the balcony were full upon me.

An ugly smile distorted the cruel lips of Matai Shang. Thurid hurled a taunt at me and placed a familiar hand upon the shoulder of my princess. Like a tigress she turned upon him, striking the beast a heavy blow with the manacles upon her wrist.

He would have struck back had not Matai Shang interfered, and then I saw that the two men were not over-friendly; for the manner of the thern was arrogant and domineering as he made it plain to the First Born that the Princess of Helium was the personal property of the Father of Therns. And Thurid's bearing toward the ancient hekkador savored not at all of liking or respect.

When the altercation in the balcony had subsided Matai Shang turned again to me.

"Earth man," he cried, "you have earned a more ignoble death than now lies within our weakened power to inflict upon you; but that the death you die tonight may be doubly bitter, know you that when you have passed, your widow becomes the wife of Matai Shang, Hekkador of the Holy Therns, for a Martian year.

"At the end of that time, as you know, she shall be discarded, as is the law among us, but not, as is usual, to lead a quiet and honored life as high priestess of some hallowed shrine. Instead, Dejah Thoris, Princess of Helium, shall become the plaything of my lieutenants—perhaps of thy most hated enemy, Thurid, the black dator."

As he ceased speaking he awaited in silence evidently for some outbreak of rage upon my part—something that would have added to the spice of his revenge. But I did not give him the satisfaction that he craved.

Instead, I did the one thing of all others that might rouse his anger and increase his hatred of me; for I knew that if I died Dejah Thoris, too, would find a way to die before they could heap further tortures or indignities upon her.

Of all the holy of holies which the thern venerates and worships none is more revered than the yellow wig which covers his bald pate, and next thereto comes the circlet of gold and the great diadem, whose scintillant rays mark the attainment of the Tenth Cycle.

And, knowing this, I removed the wig and circlet from my head, tossing them carelessly upon the flagging of the court. Then I wiped my feet upon the yellow tresses; and as a groan of rage arose from the balcony I spat full upon the holy diadem.

Matai Shang went livid with anger, but upon the lips of Thurid I could see a grim smile of amusement, for to him these things were not holy; so, lest he should derive too much amusement from my act, I cried: "And thus did I with the holies of Issus, Goddess of Life Eternal, ere I threw Issus herself to the mob that once had worshiped her, to be torn to pieces in her own temple."

That put an end to Thurid's grinning, for he had been high in the favor of Issus.

"Let us have an end to this blaspheming!" he cried, turning to the Father of Therns.

Matai Shang rose and, leaning over the edge of the balcony, gave voice to the weird call that I had heard from the lips of the priests upon the tiny balcony upon the face of the Golden Cliffs overlooking the Valley Dor, when, in times past, they called the fearsome white apes and the hideous plant men to the feast of victims floating down the broad bosom of the mysterious Iss toward the silian-infested waters of the Lost Sea of Korus.

"Let loose the death!" he cried, and immediately a dozen doors in the base of the tower swung open, and a dozen grim and terrible banths sprang into the arena.

This was not the first time that I had faced the ferocious Barsoomian lion, but never had I been pitted, single-handed, against a full dozen of them. Even with the assist-

40

ance of the fierce Woola, there could be but a single outcome to so unequal a struggle.

For a moment the beasts hesitated beneath the brilliant glare of the torches; but presently their eyes, becoming accustomed to the light, fell upon Woola and me, and with bristling manes and deep-throated roars they advanced, lashing their tawny sides with their powerful tails.

In the brief interval of life that was left me I shot a last, parting glance toward my Dejah Thoris. Her beautiful face was set in an expression of horror; and as my eyes met hers she extended both arms toward me as, struggling with the guards who now held her, she endeavored to cast herself from the balcony into the pit beneath, that she might share my death with me. Then, as the banths were about to close upon me, she turned and buried her dear face in her arms.

Suddenly my attention was drawn toward Thuvia of Ptarth. The beautiful girl was leaning far over the edge of the balcony, her eyes bright with excitement.

In another instant the banths would be upon me, but I could not force my gaze from the features of the red girl, for I knew that her expression meant anything but the enjoyment of the grim tragedy that would so soon be enacted below her; there was some deeper, hidden meaning which I sought to solve.

For an instant I thought of relying on my earthly muscles and agility to escape the banths and reach the balcony, which I could easily have done, but I could not bring myself to desert the faithful Woola and leave him to die alone beneath the cruel fangs of the hungry banths; that is not the way upon Barsoom, nor was it ever the way of John Carter.

Then the secret of Thuvia's excitement became apparent as from her lips there issued the purring sound I had heard once before; that time that, within the Golden Cliffs, she called the fierce banths about her and led them as a shepherdess might lead her flock of meek and harmless sheep.

At the first note of that soothing sound the banths halted in their tracks, and every fierce head went high as the beasts sought the origin of the familiar call. Presently they discovered the red girl in the balcony above them, and, turning, roared out their recognition and their greeting.

Guards sprang to drag Thuvia away, but ere they had succeeded she had hurled a volley of commands at the

41

listening brutes, and as one they turned and marched back into their dens.

"You need not fear them now, John Carter!" cried Thuvia, before they could silence her. "Those banths will never harm you now, nor Woola, either."

It was all I cared to know. There was naught to keep me from that balcony now, and with a long, running leap I sprang far aloft until my hands grasped its lowest sill.

In an instant all was wild confusion. Matai Shang shrank back. Thurid sprang forward with drawn sword to cut me down.

Again Dejah Thoris wielded her heavy irons and fought him back. Then Matai Shang grasped her about the waist and dragged her away through a door leading within the tower.

For an instant Thurid hesitated, and then, as though fearing that the Father of Therns would escape him with the Princess of Helium, he, too, dashed from the balcony in their wake.

Phaidor alone retained her presence of mind. Two of the guards she ordered to bear away Thuvia of Ptarth; the others she commanded to remain and prevent me from following. Then she turned toward me.

"John Carter," she cried, "for the last time I offer you the love of Phaidor, daughter of the Holy Hekkador. Accept and your princess shall be returned to the court of her grandfather, and you shall live in peace and happiness. Refuse and the fate that my father has threatened shall fall upon Dejah Thoris.

"You cannot save her now, for by this time they have reached a place where even you may not follow. Refuse and naught can save you; for, though the way to the last stronghold of the Holy Therns was made easy for you, the way hence hath been made impossible. What say you?"

"You knew my answer, Phaidor," I replied, "before ever you spoke. Make way," I cried to the guards, "for John Carter, Prince of Helium, would pass!"

With that I leaped over the low baluster that surrounded the balcony, and with drawn long-sword faced my enemies.

There were three of them; but Phaidor must have guessed what the outcome of the battle would be, for she turned and fled from the balcony the moment she saw that I would have none of her proposition.

The three guardsmen did not wait for my attack. Instead, they rushed me—the three of them simultaneously; and it was that which gave me an advantage, for they fouled one another in the narrow precincts of the balcony, so that the foremost of them stumbled full upon my blade at the first onslaught.

The red stain upon my point roused to its full the old blood-lust of the fighting man that has ever been so strong within my breast, so that my blade flew through the air with a swiftness and deadly accuracy that threw the two remaining therns into wild despair.

When at last the sharp steel found the heart of one of them the other turned to flee, and, guessing that his steps would lead him along the way taken by those I sought, I let him keep ever far enough ahead to think that he was safely escaping my sword.

Through several inner chambers he raced until he came to a spiral runway. Up this he dashed, I in close pursuit. At the upper end we came out into a small chamber, the walls of which were blank except for a single window overlooking the slopes of Otz and the Valley of Lost Souls beyond.

Here the fellow tore frantically at what appeared to be but a piece of the blank wall opposite the single window. In an instant I guessed that it was a secret exit from the room, and so I paused that he might have an opportunity to negotiate it, for I cared nothing to take the life of this poor servitor—all I craved was a clear road in pursuit of Dejah Thoris, my long-lost princess.

But, try as he would, the panel would yield neither to cunning nor force, so that eventually he gave it up and turned to face me.

"Go thy way, Thern," I said to him, pointing toward the entrance to the runway up which we had but just come. "I have no quarrel with you, nor do I crave your life. Go!"

For answer he sprang upon me with his sword, and so suddenly, at that, that I was like to have gone down before his first rush. So there was nothing for it but to give him what he sought, and that as quickly as might be, that I might not be delayed too long in this chamber while Matai Shang and Thurid made way with Dejah Thoris and Thuvia of Ptarth.

The fellow was a clever swordsman—resourceful and extremely tricky. In fact, he seemed never to have heard that there existed such a thing as a code of honor, for he repeatedly outraged a dozen Barsoomian fighting customs that an honorable man would rather die than ignore.

He even went so far as to snatch his holy wig from his head and throw it in my face, so as to blind me for a moment while he thrust at my unprotected breast.

When he thrust, however, I was not there, for I had fought with therns before; and while none had ever resorted to precisely that same expedient, I knew them to be the least honorable and most treacherous fighters upon Mars, and so was ever on the alert for some new and devilish subterfuge when I was engaged with one of their race.

But at length he overdid the thing; for, drawing his short-sword, he hurled it, javelinwise, at my body, at the same instant rushing upon me with his long-sword. A single sweeping circle of my own blade caught the flying weapon and hurled it clattering against the far wall, and then, as I sidestepped my antagonist's impetuous rush, I let him have my point full in the stomach as he hurtled by.

Clear to the hilt my weapon passed through his body, and with a frightful shriek he sank to the floor, dead.

Halting only for the brief instant that was required to wrench my sword from the carcass of my late antagonist, I sprang across the chamber to the blank wall beyond, through which the thern had attempted to pass. Here I sought for the secret of its lock, but all to no avail.

In despair I tried to force the thing, but the cold, unyielding stone might well have laughed at my futile, puny endeavors. In fact, I could have sworn that I caught the faint suggestion of taunting laughter from beyond the baffling panel.

In disgust I desisted from my useless efforts and stepped to the chamber's single window.

The slopes of Otz and the distant Valley of Lost Souls held nothing to compel my interest then; but, towering far above me, the tower's carved wall riveted my keenest attention.

Somewhere within that massive pile was Dejah Thoris. Above me I could see windows. There, possibly, lay the only way by which I could reach her. The risk was great, but not too great when the fate of a world's most wondrous woman was at stake.

I glanced below. A hundred feet beneath lay jagged granite boulders at the brink of a frightful chasm upon which the tower abutted; and if not upon the boulders, then at the chasm's bottom, lay death, should a foot slip but once, or clutching fingers loose their hold for the fraction of an instant.

But there was no other way and with a shrug, which I must admit was half shudder, I stepped to the window's outer sill and began my perilous ascent.

To my dismay I found that, unlike the ornamentation upon most Heliumetic structures, the edges of the carvings were quite generally rounded, so that at best my every hold was most precarious.

Fifty feet above me commenced a series of projecting cylindrical stones some six inches in diameter. These apparently circled the tower at six-foot intervals, in bands six feet apart; and as each stone cylinder protruded some four or five inches beyond the surface of the other ornamentation, they presented a comparatively easy mode of ascent could I but reach them.

Laboriously I climbed toward them by way of some windows which lay below them, for I hoped that I might find ingress to the tower through one of these, and thence an easier avenue along which to prosecute my search.

At times so slight was my hold upon the rounded surfaces of the carving's edges that a sneeze, a cough, or even a slight gust of wind would have dislodged me and sent me hurtling to the depths below.

But finally I reached a point where my fingers could just clutch the sill of the lowest window, and I was on the point of breathing a sigh of relief when the sound of voices came to me from above through the open window.

"He can never solve the secret of that lock." The voice was Matai Shang's. "Let us proceed to the hangar above that we may be far to the south before he finds another way—should that be possible."

"All things seem possible to that vile calot," replied another voice, which I recognized as Thurid's.

"Then let us haste," said Matai Shang. "But to be doubly sure, I will leave two who shall patrol this runway. Later they may follow us upon another flier—overtaking us at Kaol."

My upstretched fingers never reached the window's sill. At the first sound of the voices I drew back my hand and clung there to my perilous perch, flattened against the perpendicular wall, scarce daring to breathe.

What a horrible position, indeed, in which to be discovered by Thurid! He had but to lean from the window to push me with his sword's point into eternity.

Presently the sound of the voices became fainter, and once again I took up my hazardous ascent, now more difficult, since more circuitous, for I must climb so as to avoid the windows.

Matai Shang's reference to the hangar and the fliers indicated that my destination lay nothing short of the roof of the tower, and toward this seemingly distant goal I set my face.

The most difficult and dangerous part of the journey was accomplished at last, and it was with relief that I felt my fingers close about the lowest of the stone cylinders.

It is true that these projections were too far apart to make the balance of the ascent anything of a sinecure, but I at least had always within my reach a point of safety to which I might cling in case of accident.

Some ten feet below the roof, the wall inclined slightly inward possibly a foot in the last ten feet, and here the climbing was indeed immeasurably easier, so that my fingers soon clutched the eaves.

As I drew my eyes above the level of the tower's top I saw a flier all but ready to rise.

Upon her deck were Matai Shang, Phaidor, Dejah Thoris, Thuvia of Ptarth, and a few thern warriors, while near her was Thurid in the act of clambering aboard.

He was not ten paces from me, facing in the opposite direction; and what cruel freak of fate should have caused him to turn about just as my eyes topped the roof's edge I may not even guess.

But turn he did; and when his eyes met mine his wicked face lighted with a malignant smile as he leaped toward me, where I was hastening to scramble to the secure footing of the roof.

Dejah Thoris must have seen me at the same instant, for

she screamed a useless warning just as Thurid's foot, swinging in a mighty kick, landed full in my face.

Like a felled ox, I reeled and tumbled backward over the tower's side.

ON THE KAOLIAN ROAD

IF THERE be a fate that is sometimes cruel to me, there surely is a kind and merciful Providence which watches over me.

As I toppled from the tower into the horrid abyss below I counted myself already dead; and Thurid must have done likewise, for he evidently did not even trouble himself to look after me, but must have turned and mounted the waiting flier at once.

Ten feet only I fell, and then a loop of my tough, leathern harness caught upon one of the cylindrical stone projections in the tower's surface—and held. Even when I had ceased to fall I could not believe the miracle that had preserved me from instant death, and for a moment I hung there, cold sweat exuding from every pore of my body.

But when at last I had worked myself back to a firm position I hesitated to ascend, since I could not then know that Thurid was not still awaiting me above.

Presently, however, there came to my ears the whirring of the propellers of a flier, and as each moment the sound grew fainter I realized that the party had proceeded toward the south without assuring themselves as to my fate.

Cautiously I retraced my way to the roof, and I must admit that it was with no pleasant sensation that I raised my eyes once more above its edge; but, to my relief, there was no one in sight, and a moment later I stood safely upon its broad surface.

To reach the hangar and drag forth the only other flier which it contained was the work of but an instant; and just as the two thern warriors whom Matai Shang had left to prevent this very contingency emerged upon the roof from the tower's interior, I rose above them with a taunting laugh.

Then I dived rapidly to the inner court where I had last seen Woola, and to my immense relief found the faithful beast still there.

The twelve great banths lay in the doorways of their lairs, eyeing him and growling ominously, but they had not

48

disobeyed Thuvia's injunction; and I thanked the fate that had made her their keeper within the Golden Cliffs, and endowed her with the kind and sympathetic nature that had won the loyalty and affection of these fierce beasts for her.

Woola leaped in frantic joy when he discovered me; and as the flier touched the pavement of the court for a brief instant he bounded to the deck beside me, and in the bearlike manifestation of his exuberant happiness all but caused me to wreck the vessel against the courtyard's rocky wall.

Amid the angry shouting of thern guardsmen we rose high above the last fortress of the Holy Therns, and then raced straight toward the northeast and Kaol, the destination which I had heard from the lips of Matai Shang.

Far ahead, a tiny speck in the distance, I made out another flier late in the afternoon. It could be none other than that which bore my lost love and my enemies.

I had gained considerably on the craft by night; and then, knowing that they must have sighted me and would show no lights after dark, I set my destination compass upon her —that wonderful little Martian mechanism which, once attuned to the object of destination, points away toward it, irrespective of every change in its location.

All that night we raced through the Barsoomian void, passing over low hills and dead sea bottoms; above long-deserted cities and populous centers of red Martian habitation upon the ribbon-like lines of cultivated land which border the globe-encircling waterways, which Earth men call the canals of Mars.

Dawn showed that I had gained appreciably upon the flier ahead of me. It was a larger craft than mine, and not so swift; but even so, it had covered an immense distance since the flight began.

The change in vegetation below showed me that we were rapidly nearing the equator. I was now near enough to my quarry to have used my bow gun; but, though I could see that Dejah Thoris was not on deck, I feared to fire upon the craft which bore her.

Thurid was deterred by no such scruples; and though it must have been difficult for him to believe that it was really I who followed them, he could not very well doubt the witness of his own eyes; and so he trained their stern gun

49

upon me with his own hands, and an instant later an explosive radium projectile whizzed perilously close above my deck.

The black's next shot was more accurate, striking my flier full upon the prow and exploding with the instant of contact, ripping wide open the bow buoyancy tanks and disabling the engine.

So quickly did my bow drop after the shot that I scarce had time to lash Woola to the deck and buckle my own harness to a gunwale ring before the craft was hanging stern up and making her last long drop to ground.

Her stern buoyancy tanks prevented her dropping with great rapidity; but Thurid was firing rapidly now in an attempt to burst these also, that I might be dashed to death in the swift fall that would instantly follow a successful shot.

Shot after shot tore past or into us, but by a miracle neither Woola nor I was hit, nor were the after tanks punctured. This good fortune could not last indefinitely, and, assured that Thurid would not again leave me alive, I awaited the bursting of the next shell that hit; and then, throwing my hands above my head, I let go my hold and crumpled, limp and inert, dangling in my harness like a corpse.

The ruse worked, and Thurid fired no more at us. Presently I heard the diminishing sound of whirring propellers, and realized that again I was safe.

Slowly the stricken flier sank to the ground, and when I had freed myself and Woola from the entangling wreckage I found that we were upon the verge of a natural forest—so rare a thing upon the bosom of dying Mars that, outside of the forest in the Valley Dor beside the Lost Sea of Korus, I never before had seen its like upon the planet.

From books and travelers I had learned something of the little-known land of Kaol, which lies along the equator almost halfway round the planet to the east of Helium.

It comprises a sunken area of extreme tropical heat, and is inhabited by a nation of red men varying but little in manners, customs, and appearance from the balance of the red men of Barsoom.

I knew that they were among those of the outer world who still clung tenaciously to the discredited religion of the Holy Therns, and that Matai Shang would find a ready welcome and safe refuge among them; while John Carter could look for nothing better than an ignoble death at their hands.

The isolation of the Kaolians is rendered almost complete by the fact that no waterway connects their land with that of any other nation, nor have they any need of a waterway since the low, swampy land which comprises the entire area of their domain self-waters their abundant tropical crops.

For great distances in all directions rugged hills and arid stretches of dead sea bottom discourage intercourse with them, and since there is practically no such thing as foreign commerce upon warlike Barsoom, where each nation is sufficient to itself, really little has been known relative to the court of the Jeddak of Kaol and the numerous strange, but interesting, people over whom he rules.

Occasional hunting parties have traveled to this out-of-the-way corner of the globe, but the hostility of the natives has usually brought disaster upon them, so that even the sport of hunting the strange and savage creatures which haunt the jungle fastnesses of Kaol has of later years proved insufficient lure even to the most intrepid warriors.

It was upon the verge of the land of the Kaols that I now knew myself to be, but in what direction to search for Dejah Thoris, or how far into the heart of the great forest I might have to penetrate I had not the faintest idea.

But not so Woola.

Scarcely had I disentangled him than he raised his head high in air and commenced circling about at the edge of the forest. Presently he halted, and, turning to see if I were following, set off straight into the maze of trees in the direction we had been going before Thurid's shot had put an end to our flier.

As best I could, I stumbled after him down a steep declivity beginning at the forest's edge.

Immense trees reared their mighty heads far above us, their broad fronds completely shutting off the slightest glimpse of the sky. It was easy to see why the Kaolians needed no navy; their cities, hidden in the midst of this towering forest, must be entirely invisible from above, nor could a landing be made by any but the smallest fliers, and then only with the greatest risk of accident.

How Thurid and Matai Shang were to land I could not

imagine, though later I was to learn that to the level of the forest top there rises in each city of Kaol a slender watchtower which guards the Kaolians by day and by night against the secret approach of a hostile fleet. To one of these the hekkador of the Holy Therns had no difficulty in approaching, and by its means the party was safely lowered to the ground.

As Woola and I approached the bottom of the declivity the ground became soft and mushy, so that it was with the greatest difficulty that we made any headway whatever.

Slender purple grasses topped with red and yellow fernlike fronds grew rankly all about us to the height of several feet above my head.

Myriad creepers hung festooned in graceful loops from tree to tree, and among them were several varieties of the Martian "man-flower," whose blooms have eyes and hands with which to see and seize the insects which form their diet.

The repulsive calot tree was, too, much in evidence. It is a carnivorous plant of about the bigness of a large sagebrush such as dots our western plains. Each branch ends in a set of strong jaws, which have been known to drag down and devour large and formidable beasts of prey.

Both Woola and I had several narrow escapes from these greedy, arboreous monsters.

Occasional areas of firm sod gave us intervals of rest from the arduous labor of traversing this gorgeous, twilight swamp, and it was upon one of these that I finally decided to make camp for the night which my chronometer warned me would soon be upon us.

Many varieties of fruit grew in abundance about us; and as Martian calots are omnivorous, Woola had no difficulty in making a square meal after I had brought down the viands for him. Then, having eaten, too, I lay down with my back to that of my faithful hound, and dropped into a deep and dreamless sleep.

The forest was shrouded in impenetrable darkness when a low growl from Woola awakened me. All about us I could hear the stealthy movement of great, padded feet, and now and then the wicked gleam of green eyes upon us. Arising, I drew my long-sword and waited.

Suddenly a deep-toned, horried roar burst from some savage throat almost at my side. What a fool I had been not to have found safer lodgings for myself and Woola among the branches of one of the countless trees that surrounded us!

By daylight it would have been comparatively easy to have hoisted Woola aloft in one manner or another, but now it was too late. There was nothing for it but to stand our ground and take our medicine, though, from the hideous racket which now assailed our ears, and for which that first roar had seemed to be the signal, I judged that we must be in the midst of hundreds, perhaps thousands, of the fierce, man-eating denizens of the Kaolian jungle.

All the balance of the night they kept up their infernal din, but why they did not attack us I could not guess, nor am I sure to this day, unless it is that none of them ever venture upon the patches of scarlet sward which dot the swamp.

When morning broke they were still there, walking about as in a circle, but always just beyond the edge of the sward. A more terrifying aggregation of fierce and blood-thirsty monsters it would be difficult to imagine.

Singly and in pairs they commenced wandering off into the jungle shortly after sunrise, and when the last of them had departed Woola and I resumed our journey.

Occasionally we caught glimpses of horrid beasts all during the day; but, fortunately, we were never far from a sward island, and when they saw us their pursuit always ended at the verge of the solid sod.

Toward noon we stumbled upon a well-constructed road running in the general direction we had been pursuing. Everything about this highway marked it as the work of skilled engineers, and I was confident, from the indications of antiquity which it bore, as well as from the very evident signs of its being still in everyday use, that it must lead to one of the principal cities of Kaol.

Just as we entered it from one side a huge monster emerged from the jungle upon the other, and at sight of us charged madly in our direction.

Imagine, if you can, a bald-faced hornet of your earthly experience grown to the size of a prize Hereford bull, and you will have some faint conception of the ferocious appearance and awesome formidability of the winged monster that bore down upon me.

Frightful jaws in front and mighty, poisoned sting behind made my relatively puny long-sword seem a pitiful weapon of defense indeed. Nor could I hope to escape the lightning-like movements or hide from those myriad facet eyes which covered three-fourths of the hideous head, permitting the creature to see in all directions at one and the same time.

Even my powerful and ferocious Woola was as helpless as a kitten before that frightful thing. But to flee were useless, even had it ever been to my liking to turn my back upon a danger; so I stood my ground, Woola snarling at my side, my only hope to die as I had always lived—fighting.

The creature was upon us now, and at the instant there seemed to me a single slight chance for victory. If I could but remove the terrible menace of certain death hidden in the poison sacs that fed the sting the struggle would be less unequal.

At the thought I called to Woola to leap upon the creature's head and hang there, and as his mighty jaws closed upon that fiendish face, and glistening fangs buried themselves in the bone and cartilage and lower part of one of the huge eyes, I dived beneath the great body as the creature rose, dragging Woola from the ground, that it might bring its sting beneath and pierce the body of the thing hanging to its head.

To put myself in the path of that poison-laden lance was to court instant death, but it was the only way; and as the thing shot lightning-like toward me I swung my long-sword in a terrific cut that severed the deadly member close to the gorgeously marked body.

Then, like a battering-ram, one of the powerful hind legs caught me full in the chest and hurled me, half stunned and wholly winded, clear across the broad highway and into the underbrush of the jungle that fringes it.

Fortunately, I passed between the boles of trees; had I struck one of them I should have been badly injured, if not killed, so swiftly had I been catapulted by that enormous hind leg.

Dazed though I was, I stumbled to my feet and staggered back to Woola's assistance, to find his savage antagonist circling ten feet above the ground, beating madly at the clinging calot with all six powerful legs.

Even during my sudden flight through the air I had not once released my grip upon my long-sword, and now I ran beneath the two battling monsters, jabbing the winged terror repeatedly with its sharp point.

The thing might easily have risen out of my reach, but evidently it knew as little concerning retreat in the face of danger as either Woola or I, for it dropped quickly toward me, and before I could escape had grasped my shoulder between its powerful jaws.

Time and again the now useless stub of its giant sting struck futilely against my body, but the blows alone were almost as effective as the kick of a horse; so that when I say futilely, I refer only to the natural function of the disabled member—eventually the thing would have hammered me to a pulp.

Nor was it far from accomplishing this when an interruption occurred that put an end forever to its hostilities.

From where I hung a few feet above the road I could see along the highway a few hundred yards to where it turned toward the east, and just as I had about given up all hope of escaping the perilous position in which I now was I saw a red warrior come into view from around the bend.

He was mounted on a splendid thoat, one of the smaller species used by red men, and in his hand was a wondrous long, light lance.

His mount was walking sedately when I first perceived them, but the instant that the red man's eyes fell upon us a word to the thoat brought the animal at full charge down upon us. The long lance of the warrior dipped toward us, and as thoat and rider hurtled beneath, the point passed through the body of our antagonist.

With a convulsive shudder the thing stiffened, the jaws relaxed, dropping me to the ground, and then, careening once in mid air, the creature plunged headforemost to the road, full upon Woola, who still clung tenaciously to its gory head.

By the time I had regained my feet the red man had turned and ridden back to us. Woola, finding his enemy inert and lifeless, released his hold at my command and wriggled from beneath the body that had covered him, and together we faced the warrior looking down upon us.

I started to thank the stranger for his timely assistance, but he cut me off peremptorily.

"Who are you," he asked, "who dare enter the land of Kaol and hunt in the royal forest of the jeddak?"

Then, as he noted my white skin through the coating of grime and blood that covered me, his eyes went wide and in an altered tone he whispered: "Can it be that you are a Holy Thern?"

I might have deceived the fellow for a time, as I had deceived others, but I had cast away the yellow wig and the holy diadem in the presence of Matai Shang, and I knew that it would not be long ere my new aquaintance discovered that I was no thern at all.

"I am not a thern," I replied, and then, flinging caution to the winds, I said: "I am John Carter, Prince of Helium, whose name may not be entirely unknown to you."

If his eyes had gone wide when he thought that I was a Holy Thern, they fairly popped now that he knew that I was John Carter. I grasped my long-sword more firmly as I spoke the words which I was sure would precipitate an attack, but to my surprise they precipitated nothing of the kind.

"John Carter, Prince of Helium," he repeated slowly, as though he could not quite grasp the truth of the statement. "John Carter, the mightiest warrior of Barsoom!"

And then he dismounted and placed his hand upon my shoulder after the manner of most friendly greeting upon Mars.

"It is my duty, and it should be my pleasure, to kill you, John Carter," he said, "but always in my heart of hearts have I admired your prowess and believed in your sincerity the while I have questioned and disbelieved the therns and their religion.

"It would mean my instant death were my heresy to be suspected in the court of Kulan Tith, but if I may serve you, Prince, you have but to command Torkar Bar, Dwar of the Kaolian Road."

Truth and honesty were writ large upon the warrior's noble countenance, so that I could not but have trusted him, enemy though he should have been. His title of Captain of the Kaolian Road explained his timely presence in the heart of the savage forest, for every highway upon Barsoom is patrolled by doughty warriors of the noble class, nor is there any service more honorable than this lonely and dangerous duty in the less frequented sections of the domains of the red men of Barsoom.

"Torkar Bar has already placed a great debt of gratitude

upon my shoulders," I replied, pointing to the carcass of the creature from whose heart he was dragging his long spear.

The red man smiled.

"It was fortunate that I came when I did," he said. "Only this poisoned spear pricking the very heart of a sith can kill it quickly enough to save its prey. In this section of Kaol we are all armed with a long sith spear, whose point is smeared with the poison of the creature it is intended to kill; no other virus acts so quickly upon the beast as its own.

"Look," he continued, drawing his dagger and making an incision in the carcass a foot above the root of the sting, from which he presently drew forth two sacs, each of which held fully a gallon of the deadly liquid.

"Thus we maintain our supply, though were it not for certain commercial uses to which the virus is put it would scarcely be necessary to add to our present store, since the sith is almost extinct.

"Only occasionally do we now run upon one. Of old, however, Kaol was overrun with the frightful monsters that often came in herds of twenty or thirty, darting down from above into our cities and carrying away women, children, and even warriors."

As he spoke I had been wondering just how much I might safely tell this man of the mission which brought me to his land, but his next words anticipated the broaching of the subject on my part, and rendered me thankful that I had not spoken too soon.

"And now as to yourself, John Carter," he said, "I shall not ask your business here, nor do I wish to hear it. I have eyes and ears and ordinary intelligence, and yesterday morning I saw the party that came to the city of Kaol from the north in a small flier. But one thing I ask of you, and that is: the word of John Carter that he contemplates no overt act against either the nation of Kaol or its jeddak."

"You have my word as to that, Torkar Bar," I replied.

"My way leads along the Kaolian road, away from the city of Kaol," he continued. "I have seen no one—John Carter least of all. Nor have you seen Torkar Bar, nor ever heard of him. You understand?"

"Perfectly," I replied.

He laid his hand upon my shoulder.

"This road leads directly into the city of Kaol," he said. "I

57

wish you fortune," and vaulting to the back of his thoat he trotted away without even a backward glance.

It was after dark when Woola and I spied through the mighty forest the great wall which surrounds the city of Kaol.

We had traversed the entire way without mishap or adventure, and though the few we had met had eyed the great calot wonderingly, none had pierced the red pigment with which I had smoothly smeared every square inch of my body.

But to traverse the surrounding country, and to enter the guarded city of Kulan Tith, Jeddak of Kaol, were two very different things. No man enters a Martian city without giving a very detailed and satisfactory account of himself, nor did I delude myself with the belief that I could for a moment impose upon the acumen of the officers of the guard to whom I should be taken the moment I applied at any one of the gates.

My only hope seemed to lie in entering the city surreptitiously under cover of the darkness, and once in, trust to my own wits to hide myself in some crowded quarter where detection would be less liable to occur.

With this idea in view I circled the great wall, keeping within the fringe of the forest, which is cut away for a short distance from the wall all about the city, that no enemy may utilize the trees as a means of ingress.

Several times I attempted to scale the barrier at different points, but not even my earthly muscles could overcome that cleverly constructed rampart. To a height of thirty feet the face of the wall slanted outward, and then for almost an equal distance it was perpendicular, above which it slanted in again for some fifteen feet to the crest.

And smooth! Polished glass could not be more so. Finally I had to admit that at last I had discovered a Barsoomian fortification which I could not negotiate.

Discouraged, I withdrew into the forest beside a broad highway which entered the city from the east, and with Woola beside me lay down to sleep.

A HERO IN KAOL

IT WAS daylight when I was awakened by the sound of stealthy movement near by.

As I opened my eyes Woola, too, moved and, coming up to his haunches, stared through the intervening brush toward the road, each hair upon his neck stiffly erect.

At first I could see nothing, but presently I caught a glimpse of a bit of smooth and glossy green moving among the scarlet and purple and yellow of the vegetation.

Motioning Woola to remain quietly where he was, I crept forward to investigate, and from behind the bole of a great tree I saw a long line of the hideous green warriors of the dead sea bottoms hiding in the dense jungle beside the road.

As far as I could see, the silent line of destruction and death stretched away from the city of Kaol. There could be but one explanation. The green men were expecting an exodus of a body of red troops from the nearest city gate, and they were lying there in ambush to leap upon them.

I owed no fealty to the Jeddak of Kaol, but he was of the same race of noble red men as my own princess, and I would not stand supinely by and see his warriors butchered by the cruel and heartless demons of the waste places of Barsoom.

Cautiously I retraced my steps to where I had left Woola, and warning him to silence, signaled him to follow me. Making a considerable detour to avoid the chance of falling into the hands of the green men, I came at last to the great wall.

A hundred yards to my right was the gate from which the troops were evidently expected to issue, but to reach it I must pass the flank of the green warriors within easy sight of them, and, fearing that my plan to warn the Kaolians might thus be thwarted, I decided upon hastening toward the left, where another gate a mile away would give me ingress to the city.

I knew that the word I brought would prove a splendid passport to Kaol, and I must admit that my caution was due more to my ardent desire to make my way into the city than to avoid a brush with the green men. As much as I enjoy a fight, I cannot always indulge myself, and just now I had more weighty matters to occupy my time than spilling the blood of strange warriors.

Could I but win beyond the city's wall, there might be opportunity in the confusion and excitement which were sure to follow my announcement of an invading force of green warriors to find my way within the palace of the jeddak, where I was sure Matai Shang and his party would be quartered.

But scarcely had I taken a hundred steps in the direction of the farther gate when the sound of marching troops, the clank of metal, and the squealing of thoats just within the city apprised me of the fact that the Kaolians were already moving toward the other gate.

There was no time to be lost. In another moment the gate would be opened and the head of the column pass out upon the death-bordered highway.

Turning back toward the fateful gate, I ran rapidly along the edge of the clearing, taking the ground in the mighty leaps that had first made me famous upon Barsoom. Thirty, fifty, a hundred feet at a bound are nothing for the muscles of an athletic Earth man upon Mars.

As I passed the flank of the waiting green men they saw my eyes turned upon them, and in an instant, knowing that all secrecy was at an end, those nearest me sprang to their feet in an effort to cut me off before I could reach the gate.

At the same instant the mighty portal swung wide and the head of the Kaolian column emerged. A dozen green warriors had succeeded in reaching a point between me and the gate, but they had but little idea who it was they had elected to detain.

I did not slacken my speed an iota as I dashed among them, and as they fell before my blade I could not but recall the happy memory of those other battles when Tars Tarkas, Jeddak of Thark, mightiest of Martian green men, had stood shoulder to shoulder with me through long, hot Martian days, as together we hewed down our enemies until the pile of corpses about us rose higher than a tall man's head.

When several pressed me too closely, there before the carved gateway of Kaol, I leaped above their heads, and fashioning my tactics after those of the hideous plant men of Dor, struck down upon my enemies' heads as I passed above them.

From the city the red warriors were rushing toward us, and from the jungle the savage horde of green men were coming to meet them. In a moment I was in the very center of as fierce and bloody a battle as I had ever passed through.

These Kaolians are most noble fighters, nor are the green men of the equator one whit less warlike than their cold, cruel cousins of the temperate zone. There were many times when either side might have withdrawn without dishonor and thus ended hostilities, but from the mad abandon with which each invariably renewed hostilities I soon came to believe that what need not have been more than a trifling skirmish would end only with the complete extermination of one force or the other.

With the joy of battle once roused within me, I took keen delight in the fray, and that my fighting was noted by the Kaolians was often evidenced by the shouts of applause directed at me.

If I sometimes seem to take too great pride in my fighting ability, it must be remembered that fighting is my vocation. If your vocation be shoeing horses, or painting pictures, and you can do one or the other better than your fellows, then you are a fool if you are not proud of your ability. And so I am very proud that upon two planets no greater fighter has ever lived than John Carter, Prince of Helium.

And I outdid myself that day to impress the fact upon the natives of Kaol, for I wished to win a way into their hearts—and their city. Nor was I to be disappointed in my desire.

All day we fought, until the road was red with blood and clogged with corpses. Back and forth along the slippery highway the tide of battle surged, but never once was the gateway to Kaol really in danger.

There were breathing spells when I had a chance to converse with the red men beside whom I fought, and once the jeddak, Kulan Tith himself, laid his hand upon my shoulder and asked my name.

"I am Dotar Sojat," I replied, recalling a name given me by the Tharks many years before, from the surnames of the first two of their warriors I had killed, which is the custom among them.

61

"You are a mighty warrior, Dotar Sojat," he replied, "and when this day is done I shall speak with you again in the great audience chamber."

And then the fight surged upon us once more and we were separated, but my heart's desire was attained, and it was with renewed vigor and a joyous soul that I laid about me with my long-sword until the last of the green men had had enough and had withdrawn toward their distant sea bottom.

Not until the battle was over did I learn why the red troops had sallied forth that day. It seemed that Kulan Tith was expecting a visit from a mighty jeddak of the north—a powerful and the only ally of the Kaolians, and it had been his wish to meet his guest a full day's journey from Kaol.

But now the march of the welcoming host was delayed until the following morning, when the troops again set out from Kaol. I had not been bidden to the presence of Kulan Tith after the battle, but he had sent an officer to find me and escort me to comfortable quarters in that part of the palace set aside for the officers of the royal guard.

There, with Woola, I had spent a comfortable night, and rose much refreshed after the arduous labors of the past few days. Woola had fought with me through the battle of the previous day, true to the instincts and training of a Martian war dog, great numbers of which are often to be found with the savage green hordes of the dead sea bottoms.

Neither of us had come through the conflict unscathed, but the marvelous, healing salves of Barsoom had sufficed, overnight, to make us as good as new.

I breakfasted with a number of the Kaolian officers, whom I found as courteous and delightful hosts as even the nobles of Helium, who are renowned for their ease of manners and excellence of breeding. The meal was scarcely concluded when a messenger arrived from Kulan Tith summoning me before him.

As I entered the royal presence the jeddak rose, and stepping from the dais which supported his magnificent throne, came forward to meet me—a mark of distinction that is seldom accorded to other than a visiting ruler.

"Kaor, Dotar Sojat!" he greeted me. "I have summoned you to receive the grateful thanks of the people of Kaol, for had it not been for your heroic bravery in daring fate to warn us of the ambuscade we must surely have fallen into the well-laid trap. Tell me more of yourself—from what country you come, and what errand brings you to the court of Kulan Tith."

"I am from Hastor," I said, for in truth I had a small palace in that southern city which lies within the far-flung dominions of the Heliumetic nation.

"My presence in the land of Kaol is partly due to accident, my flier being wrecked upon the southern fringe of your great forest. It was while seeking entrance to the city of Kaol that I discovered the green horde lying in wait for your troops."

If Kulan Tith wondered what business brought me in a flier to the very edge of his domain he was good enough not to press me further for an explanation, which I should indeed have had difficulty in rendering.

During my audience with the jeddak another party entered the chamber from behind me, so that I did not see their faces until Kulan Tith stepped past me to greet them, commanding me to follow and be presented.

As I turned toward them it was with difficulty that I controlled my features, for there, listening to Kulan Tith's eulogistic words concerning me, stood my arch-enemies, Matai Shang and Thurid.

"Holy Hekkador of the Holy Therns," the jeddak was saying, "shower thy blessings upon Dotar Sojat, the valorous stranger from distant Hastor, whose wondrous heroism and marvelous ferocity saved the day for Kaol yesterday."

Matai Shang stepped forward and laid his hand upon my shoulder. No slightest indication that he recognized me showed upon his countenance—my disguise was evidently complete.

He spoke kindly to me and then presented me to Thurid. The black, too, was evidently entirely deceived. Then Kulan Tith regaled them, much to my amusement, with details of my achievements upon the field of battle.

The thing that seemed to have impressed him most was my remarkable agility, and time and again he described the wondrous way in which I had leaped completely over an antagonist, cleaving his skull wide open with my long-sword as I passed above him.

I thought that I saw Thurid's eyes widen a bit during the narrative, and several times I surprised him gazing intently into my face through narrowed lids. Was he commencing to suspect? And then Kulan Tith told of the savage calot that fought beside me, and after that I saw suspicion in the eyes of Matai Shang—or did I but imagine it?

At the close of the audience Kulan Tith announced that he would have me accompany him upon the way to meet his royal guest, and as I departed with an officer who was to procure proper trappings and a suitable mount for me, both Matai Shang and Thurid seemed most sincere in professing their pleasure at having had an opportunity to know me. It was with a sigh of relief that I quitted the chamber, convinced that nothing more than a guilty conscience had prompted my belief that either of my enemies suspected my true identity.

A half-hour later I rode out of the city gate with the column that accompanied Kulan Tith upon the way to meet his friend and ally. Though my eyes and ears had been wide open during my audience with the jeddak and my various passages through the palace, I had seen or heard nothing of Dejah Thoris or Thuvia of Ptarth. That they must be somewhere within the great rambling edifice I was positive, and I should have given much to have found a way to remain behind during Kulan Tith's absence, that I might search for them.

Toward noon we came in touch with the head of the column we had set out to meet.

It was a gorgeous train that accompanied the visiting jeddak, and for miles it stretched along the wide, white road to Kaol. Mounted troops, their trappings of jewel and metal-incrusted leather glistening in the sunlight, formed the vanguard of the body, and then came a thousand gorgeous chariots drawn by huge zitidars.

These low, commodious wagons moved two abreast, and on either side of them marched solid ranks of mounted warriors, for in the chariots were the women and children of the royal court. Upon the back of each monster zitidar rode a Martian youth, and the whole scene carried me back to my first days upon Barsoom, now twenty-two years in the past, when I had first beheld the gorgeous spectacle of a caravan of the green horde of Tharks.

Never before today had I seen zitidars in the service of red men. These brutes are huge mastodonian animals that tower to an immense height even beside the giant green men and

64

their giant thoats; but when compared to the relatively small red man and his breed of thoats they assume Brobdingnagian proportions that are truly appalling.

The beasts were hung with jeweled trappings and saddle-pads of gay silk, embroidered in fanciful designs with strings of diamonds, pearls, rubies, emeralds, and the countless unnamed jewels of Mars, while from each chariot rose a dozen standards from which streamers, flags, and pennons fluttered in the breeze.

Just in front of the chariots the visiting jeddak rode alone upon a pure white thoat—another unusual sight upon Barsoom—and after them came interminable ranks of mounted spearmen, riflemen, and swordsmen. It was indeed a most imposing sight.

Except for the clanking of accouterments and the occasional squeal of an angry thoat or the low guttural of a zitidar, the passage of the cavalcade was almost noiseless, for neither thoat nor zitidar is a hoofed animal, and the broad tires of the chariots are of an elastic composition, which gives forth no sound.

Now and then the gay laughter of a woman or the chatter of children could be heard, for the red Martians are a social, pleasure-loving people—in direct antithesis to the cold and morbid race of green men.

The forms and ceremonials connected with the meeting of the two jeddaks consumed an hour, and then we turned and retraced our way toward the city of Kaol, which the head of the column reached just before dark, though it must have been nearly morning before the rear guard passed through the gateway.

Fortunately, I was well up toward the head of the column, and after the great banquet, which I attended with the officers of the royal guard, I was free to seek repose. There was so much activity and bustle about the palace all during the night with the constant arrival of the noble officers of the visiting jeddak's retinue that I dared not attempt to prosecute a search for Dejah Thoris, and so, as soon as it was seemly for me to do so, I returned to my quarters.

As I passed along the corridors between the banquet hall and the apartments that had been allotted me, I had a sudden feeling that I was under surveillance, and, turning quickly in my tracks, caught a glimpse of a figure which darted into an open doorway the instant I wheeled about.

Though I ran quickly back to the spot where the shadower had disappeared I could find no trace of him, yet in the brief glimpse that I had caught I could have sworn that I had seen a white face surmounted by a mass of yellow hair.

The incident gave me considerable food for speculation, since if I were right in the conclusion induced by the cursory glimpse I had had of the spy, then Matai Shang and Thurid must suspect my identity, and if that were true not even the service I had rendered Kulan Tith could save me from his religious fantacisim.

But never did vague conjecture or fruitless fears for the future lie with sufficient weight upon my mind to keep me from my rest, and so tonight I threw myself upon my sleeping silks and furs and passed at once into dreamless slumber.

Calots are not permitted within the walls of the palace proper, and so I had had to relegate poor Woola to quarters in the stables where the royal thoats are kept. He had comfortable even luxurious apartments, but I would have given much to have had him with me; and if he had been, the thing which happened that night would not have come to pass.

I could not have slept over a quarter of an hour when I was suddenly awakened by the passing of some cold and clammy thing across my forehead. Instantly I sprang to my feet, clutching in the direction I thought the presence lay. For an instant my hand touched against human flesh, and then, as I lunged headforemost through the darkness to seize my nocturnal visitor, my foot became entangled in my sleeping silks and I fell sprawling to the floor.

By the time I had resumed my feet and found the button which controlled the light my caller had disappeared. Careful search of the room revealed nothing to explain either the identity or business of the person who had thus secretly sought me in the dead of night.

That the purpose might be theft I could not believe, since thieves are practically unknown upon Barsoom. Assassination, however, is rampant, but even this could not have been the motive of my stealthy friend, for he might easily have killed me had he desired.

I had about given up fruitless conjecture and was on the point of returning to sleep when a dozen Kaolian guardsmen entered my apartment. The officer in charge was one of my genial hosts of the morning, but now upon his face was no sign of friendship.

"Kulan Tith commands your presence before him," he said. "Come!"

Surrounded by guardsmen I marched back along the corridors of the palace of Kulan Tith, Jeddak of Kaol, to the great audience chamber in the center of the massive structure.

As I entered the brilliantly lighted apartment, filled with the nobles of Kaol and the officers of the visiting jeddak, all eyes were turned upon me. Upon the great dais at the end of the chamber stood three thrones, upon which sat Kulan Tith and his two guests, Matai Shang, and the visiting jeddak.

Up the broad center aisle we marched beneath deadly silence, and at the foot of the thrones we halted.

"Prefer thy charge," said Kulan Tith, turning to one who stood among the nobles at his right; and then Thurid, the black dator of the First Born, stepped forward and faced me.

"Most noble Jeddak," he said, addressing Kulan Tith, "from the first I suspected this stranger within thy palace. Your description of his fiendish prowess tallied with that of the arch-enemy of truth upon Barsoom.

"But that there might be no mistake I despatched a priest of your own holy cult to make the test that should pierce his disguise and reveal the truth. Behold the result!" and Thurid pointed a rigid finger at my forehead.

All eyes followed the direction of that accusing digit—I alone seemed at a loss to guess what fatal sign rested upon my brow.

The officer beside me guessed my perplexity; and as the brows of Kulan Tith darkened in a menacing scowl as his eyes rested upon me, the noble drew a small mirror from his pocket-pouch and held it before my face.

One glance at the reflection it gave back to me was sufficient.

From my forehead the hand of the sneaking thern had reached out through the concealing darkness of my bed-

68

chamber and wiped away a patch of the disguising red pigment as broad as my palm. Beneath showed the tanned texture of my own white skin.

For a moment Thurid ceased speaking, to enhance, I suspect, the dramatic effect of his disclosure. Then he resumed.

"Here, O Kulan Tith," he cried, "is he who has desecrated the temples of the Gods of Mars, who has violated the persons of the Holy Therns themselves and turned a world against its age-old religion. Before you, in your power, Jeddak of Kaol, Defender of the Holies, stands John Carter, Prince of Helium!"

Kulan Tith looked toward Matai Shang as though for corroboration of these charges. The Holy Thern nodded his head.

"It is indeed the arch-blasphemer," he said. "Even now he has followed me to the very heart of thy palace, Kulan Tith, for the sole purpose of assassinating me. He——"

"He lies!" I cried. "Kulan Tith, listen that you may know the truth. Listen while I tell you why John Carter has followed Matai Shang to the heart of thy palace. Listen to me as well as to them, and then judge if my acts be not more in accord with true Barsoomian chivalry and honor than those of these revengeful devotees of the spurious creeds from whose cruel bonds I have freed your planet."

"Silence!" roared the jeddak, leaping to his feet and laying his hand upon the hilt of his sword. "Silence, blasphemer! Kulan Tith need not permit the air of his audience chamber to be defiled by the heresies that issue from your polluted throat to judge you.

"You stand already self-condemned. It but remains to determine the manner of your death. Even the service that you rendered the arms of Kaol shall avail you naught; it was but a base subterfuge whereby you might win your way into my favor and reach the side of this holy man whose life you craved. To the pits with him!" he concluded, addressing the officer of my guard.

Here was a pretty pass, indeed! What chance had I against a whole nation? What hope for me of mercy at the hands of the fanatical Kulan Tith with such advisers as Matai Shang and Thurid. The black grinned malevolently in my face.

"You shall not escape this time, Earth man," he taunted.

The guards closed toward me. A red haze blurred my

vision. The fighting blood of my Virginian sires coursed hot through my veins. The lust of battle in all its mad fury was upon me.

With a leap I was beside Thurid, and ere the devilish smirk had faded from his handsome face I had caught him full upon the mouth with my clenched fist; and as the good, old American blow landed, the black dator shot back a dozen feet, to crumple in a broken heap at the foot of Kulan Tith's throne, spitting blood and teeth from his hurt mouth.

Then I drew my sword and swung round, on guard, to face a nation.

In an instant the guardsmen were upon me, but before a blow had been struck a mighty voice rose above the din of shouting warriors, and a giant figure leaped from the dais beside Kulan Tith and, with drawn long-sword, threw himself between me and my adversaries.

It was the visiting jeddak.

"Hold!" he cried. "If you value my friendship, Kulan Tith, and the age-old peace that has existed between our peoples, call off your swordsmen; for wherever or against whomsoever fights John Carter, Prince of Helium, there beside him and to the death fights Thuvan Dihn, Jeddak of Ptarth."

The shouting ceased and the menacing points were lowered as a thousand eyes turned first toward Thuvan Dihn in surprise and then toward Kulan Tith in question. At first the Jeddak of Kaol went white in rage, but before he spoke he had mastered himself, so that his tone was calm and even as befitted intercourse between two great jeddaks.

"Thuvan Dihn," he said slowly, "must have great provocation thus to desecrate the ancient customs which inspire the deportment of a guest within the palace of his host. Lest I, too, should forget myself as has my royal friend, I should prefer to remain silent until the Jeddak of Ptarth has won from me applause for his action by relating the causes which provoked it."

I could see that the Jeddak of Ptarth was of half a mind to throw his metal in Kulan Tith's face, but he controlled himself even as well as had his host.

"None knows better than Thuvan Dihn," he said, "the laws which govern the acts of men in the domains of their neighbors; but Thuvan Dihn owes allegiance to a higher law than these—the law of gratitude. Nor to any man upon Barsoom does he owe a greater debt of gratitude than to John Carter, Prince of Helium.

"Years ago, Kulan Tith," he continued, "upon the occasion of your last visit to me, you were greatly taken with the charms and graces of my only daughter, Thuvia. You saw how I adored her, and later you learned that, inspired by some unfathomable whim, she had taken the last, long, voluntary pilgrimage upon the cold bosom of the mysterious Iss, leaving me desolate.

"Some months ago I first heard of the expedition which John Carter had led against Issus and the Holy Therns. Faint rumors of the atrocities reported to have been committed by the therns upon those who for countless ages have floated down the mighty Iss came to my ears.

"I heard that thousands of prisoners had been released, few of whom dared to return to their own countries owing to the mandate of terrible death which rests against all who return from the Valley Dor.

"For a time I could not believe the heresies which I heard, and I prayed that my daughter Thuvia might have died before she ever committed the sacrilege of returning to the outer world. But then my father's love asserted itself, and I vowed that I would prefer eternal damnation to further separation from her if she could be found.

"So I sent emissaries to Helium, and to the court of Xodar, Jeddak of the First Born, and to him who now rules those of the thern nation that have renounced their religion; and from each and all I heard the same story of unspeakable cruelties and atrocities perpetrated upon the poor defenseless victims of their religion by the Holy Therns.

"Many there were who had seen or known my daughter, and from therns who had been close to Matai Shang I learned of the indignities that he personally heaped upon her; and I was glad when I came here to find that Matai Shang was also your guest, for I should have sought him out had it taken a lifetime.

"More, too, I heard, and that of the chivalrous kindness that John Carter had accorded my daughter. They told me how he fought for her and rescued her, and how he spurned escape from the savage Warhoons of the south, send-

71

ing her to safety upon his own thoat and remaining upon foot to meet the green warriors.

"Can you wonder, Kulan Tith, that I am willing to jeopardize my life, the peace of my nation, or even your friendship, which I prize more than aught else, to champion the Prince of Helium?"

For a moment Kulan Tith was silent. I could see by the expression of his face that he was sore perplexed. Then he spoke.

"Thuvan Dihn," he said, and his tone was friendly though sad, "who am I to judge my fellow-man? In my eyes the Father of Therns is still holy, and the religion which he teaches the only true religion, but were I faced by the same problem that has vexed you I doubt not that I should feel and act precisely as you have.

"In so far as the Prince of Helium is concerned I may act, but between you and Matai Shang my only office can be one of conciliation. The Prince of Helium shall be escorted in safety to the boundary of my domain ere the sun has set again, where he shall be free to go whither he will; but upon pain of death must he never again enter the land of Kaol.

"If there be a quarrel between you and the Father of Therns, I need not ask that the settlement of it be deferred until both have passed beyond the limits of my power. Are you satisfied, Thuvan Dihn?"

The Jeddak of Ptarth nodded his assent, but the ugly scowl that he bent upon Matai Shang harbored ill for that pasty-faced godling.

"The Prince of Helium is far from satisfied," I cried, breaking rudely in upon the beginnings of peace, for I had no stomach for peace at the price that had been named.

"I have escaped death in a dozen forms to follow Matai Shang and overtake him, and I do not intend to be led, like a decrepit thoat to the slaughter, from the goal that I have won by the prowess of my sword arm and the might of my muscles.

"Nor will Thuvan Dihn, Jeddak of Ptarth, be satisfied when he has heard me through. Do you know why I have followed Matai Shang and Thurid, the black dator, from the forests of the Valley Dor across half a world through almost insurmountable difficulties?

"Think you that John Carter, Prince of Helium, would

stoop to assassination? Can Kulan Tith be such a fool as to believe that lie, whispered in his ear by the Holy Thern or Dator Thurid?

"I do not follow Matai Shang to kill him, though the God of mine own planet knows that my hands itch to be at his throat. I follow him, Thuvan Dihn, because with him are two prisoners—my wife, Dejah Thoris, Princess of Helium, and your daughter, Thuvia of Ptarth.

"Now think you that I shall permit myself to be led beyond the walls of Kaol unless the mother of my son accompanies me, and thy daughter be restored?"

Thuvan Dihn turned upon Kulan Tith. Rage flamed in his keen eyes; but by the masterfulness of his self-control he kept his tones level as he spoke.

"Knew you this thing, Kulan Tith?" he asked. "Knew you that my daughter lay a prisoner in your palace?"

"He could not know it," interrupted Matai Shang, white with what I am sure was more fear than rage. "He could not know it, for it is a lie."

I would have had his life for that upon the spot, but even as I sprang toward him Thuvan Dihn laid a heavy hand upon my shoulder.

"Wait," he said to me, and then to Kulan Tith. "It is not a lie. This much have I learned of the Prince of Helium—he does not lie. Answer me, Kulan Tith—I have asked you a question."

"Three women came with the Father of Therns," replied Kulan Tith. "Phaidor, his daughter, and two who were reported to be her slaves. If these be Thuvia of Ptarth and Dejah Thoris of Helium I did not know it—I have seen neither. But if they be, then shall they be returned to you on the morrow."

As he spoke he looked straight at Matai Shang, not as a devotee should look at a high priest, but as a ruler of men looks at one to whom he issues a command.

It must have been plain to the Father of Therns, as it was to me, that the recent disclosures of his true character had done much already to weaken the faith of Kulan Tith, and that it would require but little more to turn the powerful jeddak into an avowed enemy; but so strong are the seeds of superstition that even the great Kaolian still hesitated to cut the final strand that bound him to his ancient religion.

73

Matai Shang was wise enough to seem to accept the mandate of his follower, and promised to bring the two slave women to the audience chamber on the morrow.

"It is almost morning now," he said, "and I should dislike to break in upon the slumber of my daughter, or I would have them fetched at once that you might see that the Prince of Helium is mistaken," and he emphasized the last word in an effort to affront me so subtilely that I could not take open offense.

I was about to object to any delay, and demand that the Princess of Helium be brought to me forthwith, when Thuvan Dihn made such insistence seem unnecessary.

"I should like to see my daughter at once," he said, "but if Kulan Tith will give me his assurance that none will be permitted to leave the palace this night, and that no harm shall befall either Dejah Thoris or Thuvia of Ptarth between now and the moment that they are brought into our presence in this chamber at daylight I shall not insist."

"None shall leave the palace tonight," replied the Jeddak of Kaol, "and Matai Shang will give us assurance that no harm will come to the two women?"

The thern assented with a nod. A few moments later Kulan Tith indicated that the audience was at an end, and at Thuvan Dihn's invitation I accompanied the Jeddak of Ptarth to his own apartments, where we sat until daylight, while he listened to the account of my experiences upon his planet and to all that had befallen his daughter during the time that we had been together.

I found the father of Thuvia a man after my own heart, and that night saw the beginning of a friendship which has grown until it is second only to that which obtains between Tars Tarkas, the green Jeddak of Thark, and myself.

The first burst of Mars's sudden dawn brought messengers from Kulan Tith, summoning us to the audience chamber where Thuvan Dihn was to receive his daughter after years of separation, and I was to be reunited with the glorious daughter of Helium after an almost unbroken separation of twelve years.

My heart pounded within my bosom until I looked about me in embarrassment, so sure was I that all within the room must hear. My arms ached to enfold once more the divine

74

form of her whose eternal youth and undying beauty were but outward manifestations of a perfect soul.

At last the messenger despatched to fetch Matai Shang returned. I craned my neck to catch the first glimpse of those who should be following, but the messenger was alone.

Halting before the throne he addressed his jeddak in a voice that was plainly audible to all within the chamber.

"O Kulan Tith, Mightiest of Jeddaks," he cried, after the fashion of the court, "your messenger returns alone, for when he reached the apartments of the Father of Therns he found them empty, as were those occupied by his suite."

Kulan Tith went white.

A low groan burst from the lips of Thuvan Dihn who stood next me, not having ascended the throne which awaited him beside his host. For a moment the silence of death reigned in the great audience chamber of Kulan Tith, Jeddak of Kaol. It was he who broke the spell.

Rising from his throne he stepped down from the dais to the side of Thuvan Dihn. Tears dimmed his eyes as he placed both his hands upon the shoulders of his friend.

"O Thuvan Dihn," he cried, "that this should have happened in the palace of thy best friend! With my own hands would I have wrung the neck of Matai Shang had I guessed what was in his foul heart. Last night my life-long faith was weakened—this morning it has been shattered; but too late, too late.

"To wrest your daughter and the wife of this royal warrior from the clutches of these archfiends you have but to command the resources of a mighty nation, for all Kaol is at your disposal. What may be done? Say the word!"

"First," I suggested, "let us find those of your people who be responsible for the escape of Matai Shang and his followers. Without assistance on the part of the palace guard this thing could not have come to pass. Seek the guilty, and from them force an explanation of the manner of their going and the direction they have taken."

Before Kulan Tith could issue the commands that would initiate the investigation a handsome young officer stepped forward and addressed his jeddak.

"O Kulan Tith, Mightiest of Jeddaks," he said, "I alone be responsible for this grievous error. Last night it was I

75

who commanded the palace guard. I was on duty in other parts of the palace during the audience of the early morning, and knew nothing of what transpired then, so that when the Father of Therns summoned me and explained that it was your wish that his party be hastened from the city because of the presence here of a deadly enemy who sought the Holy Hekkador's life I did only what a lifetime of training has taught me was the proper thing to do—I obeyed him whom I believed to be the ruler of us all, mightier even than thou, mightiest of jeddaks.

"Let the consequences and the punishment fall on me alone, for I alone am guilty. Those others of the palace guard who assisted in the flight did so under my instructions."

Kulan Tith looked first at me and then at Thuvan Dihn, as though to ask our judgment upon the man, but the error was so evidently excusable that neither of us had any mind to see the young officer suffer for a mistake that any might readily have made.

"How left they," asked Thuvan Dihn, "and what direction did they take?"

"They left as they came," replied the officer, "upon their own flier. For some time after they had departed I watched the vessel's lights, which vanished finally due north."

"Where north could Matai Shang find an asylum?" asked Thuvan Dihn of Kulan Tith.

For some moments the Jeddak of Kaol stood with bowed head, apparently deep in thought. Then a sudden light brightened his countenance.

"I have it!" he cried. "Only yesterday Matai Shang let drop a hint of his destination, telling me of a race of people unlike ourselves who dwell far to the north. They, he said, had always been known to the Holy Therns and were devout and faithful followers of the ancient cult. Among them would he find a perpetual haven of refuge, where no 'lying heretics' might seek him out. It is there that Matai Shang has gone."

"And in all Kaol there be no flier wherein to follow," I cried.

"Nor nearer than Ptarth," replied Thuvan Dihn.

"Wait!" I exclaimed, "beyond the southern fringe of this great forest lies the wreck of the thern flier which brought me that far upon my way. If you will loan me men to fetch

76

it, and artificers to assist me, I can repair it in two days, Kulan Tith."

I had been more than half suspicious of the seeming sincerity of the Kaolian jeddak's sudden apostasy, but the alacrity with which he embraced my suggestion, and the despatch with which a force of officers and men were placed at my disposal entirely removed the last vestige of my doubts.

Two days later the flier rested upon the top of the watch-tower, ready to depart. Thuvan Dihn and Kulan Tith had offered me the entire resources of two nations—millions of fighting men were at my disposal; but my flier could hold but one other than myself and Woola.

As I stepped aboard her, Thuvan Dihn took his place beside me. I cast a look of questioning surprise upon him. He turned to the highest of his own officers who had accompanied him to Kaol.

"To you I entrust the return of my retinue to Ptarth," he said. "There my son rules ably in my absence. The Prince of Helium shall not go alone into the land of his enemies. I have spoken. Farewell!"

STRAIGHT toward the north, day and night, our destination compass led us after the fleeing flier upon which it had remained set since I first attuned it after leaving the thern fortress.

Early in the second night we noticed the air becoming perceptibly colder, and from the distance we had come from the equator were assured that we were rapidly approaching the north arctic region.

My knowledge of the efforts that had been made by countless expeditions to explore that unknown land bade me to caution, for never had flier returned who had passed to any considerable distance beyond the mighty ice-barrier that fringes the southern hem of the frigid zone.

What became of them none knew—only that they passed forever out of the sight of man into that grim and mysterious country of the pole.

The distance from the barrier to the pole was no more than a swift flier should cover in a few hours, and so it was assumed that some frightful catastrophe awaited those who reached the "forbidden land," as it had come to be called by the Martians of the outer world.

Thus it was that I went more slowly as we approached the barrier, for it was my intention to move cautiously by day over the ice-pack that I might discover, before I had run into a trap, if there really lay an inhabited country at the north pole, for there only could I imagine a spot where Matai Shang might feel secure from John Carter, Prince of Helium.

We were flying at a snail's pace but a few feet above the ground—literally feeling our way along through the darkness, for both moons had set, and the night was black with the clouds that are to be found only at Mars's two extremities.

Suddenly a towering wall of white rose directly in our

path, and though I threw the helm hard over, and reversed our engine, I was too late to avoid collision.

With a sickening crash we struck the high looming obstacle three-quarters on.

The flier reeled half over; the engine stopped; as one, the patched buoyancy tanks burst, and we plunged, headforemost, to the ground twenty feet beneath.

Fortunately none of us was injured, and when we had disentangled ourselves from the wreckage, and the lesser moon had burst again from below the horizon, we found that we were at the foot of a mighty ice-barrier, from which outcropped great patches of the granite hills which hold it from encroaching farther toward the south.

What fate! With the journey all but completed to be thus wrecked upon the wrong side of that precipitous and unscalable wall of rock and ice!

I looked at Thuvan Dihn. He but shook his head dejectedly.

The balance of the night we spent shivering in our inadequate sleeping silks and furs upon the snow that lies at the foot of the ice-barrier.

With daylight my battered spirits regained something of their accustomed hopefulness, though I must admit that there was little enough for them to feed upon.

"What shall we do?" asked Thuvan Dihn. "How may we pass that which is impassable?"

"First we must disprove its impassability," I replied. "Nor shall I admit that it is impassable before I have followed its entire circle and stand again upon this spot, defeated. The sooner we start, the better, for I see no other way, and it will take us more than a month to travel the weary, frigid miles that lie before us."

For five days of cold and suffering and privation we traversed the rough and frozen way which lies at the foot of the ice-barrier. Fierce, fur-bearing creatures attacked us by daylight and by dark. Never for a moment were we safe from the sudden charge of some huge demon of the north.

The apt was our most consistent and dangerous foe.

It is a huge, white-furred creature with six limbs, four of which, short and heavy, carry it swiftly over the snow and ice; while the other two, growing forward from its shoulders on either side of its long, powerful neck, terminate in

79

white, hairless hands, with which it seizes and holds its prey.

Its head and mouth are more similar in appearance to those of a hippopotamus than to any other earthly animal, except that from the sides of the lower jawbone two mighty horns curve slightly downward toward the front.

Its two huge eyes inspired my greatest curiosity. They extend in two vast, oval patches from the center of the top of the cranium down either side of the head to below the roots of the horns, so that these weapons really grow out from the lower part of the eyes, which are composed of several thousand ocelli each.

This eye structure seemed remarkable in a beast whose haunts were upon a glaring field of ice and snow, and though I found upon minute examination of several that we killed that each ocellus is furnished with its own lid, and that the animal can at will close as many of the facets of his huge eyes as he chooses, yet I was positive that nature had thus equipped him because much of his life was to be spent in dark, subterranean recesses.

Shortly after this we came upon the hugest apt that we had seen. The creature stood fully eight feet at the shoulder, and was so sleek and clean and glossy that I could have sworn that he had but recently been groomed.

He stood head-on eyeing us as we approached him, for we had found it a waste of time to attempt to escape the perpetual bestial rage which seems to possess these demon creatures, who rove the dismal north attacking every living thing that comes within the scope of their far-seeing eyes.

Even when their bellies are full and they can eat no more, they kill purely for the pleasure which they derive from taking life, and so when this particular apt failed to charge us, and instead wheeled and trotted away as we neared him, I should have been greatly surprised had I not chanced to glimpse the sheen of a golden collar about its neck.

Thuvan Dihn saw it, too, and it carried the same message of hope to us both. Only man could have placed that collar there, and as no race of Martians of which we knew aught ever had attempted to domesticate the ferocious apt, he must belong to a people of the north of whose very existence we were ignorant—possibly to the fabled yellow men of Barsoom; that once powerful race which was supposed to be extinct, though sometimes, by theorists, thought still to exist in the frozen north.

Simultaneously we started upon the trail of the great beast. Woola was quickly made to understand our desires, so that it was unnecessary to attempt to keep in sight of the animal whose swift flight over the rough ground soon put him beyond our vision.

For the better part of two hours the trail paralleled the barrier, and then suddenly turned toward it through the roughest and seemingly most impassable country I ever had beheld.

Enormous granite boulders blocked the way on every hand; deep rifts in the ice threatened to engulf us at the least misstep; and from the north a slight breeze wafted to our nostrils an unspeakable stench that almost choked us.

For another two hours we were occupied in traversing a few hundred yards to the foot of the barrier.

Then, turning about the corner of a wall-like outcropping of granite, we came upon a smooth area of two or three acres before the base of the towering pile of ice and rock that had baffled us for days, and before us beheld the dark and cavernous mouth of a cave.

From this repelling portal the horrid stench was emanating, and as Thuvan Dihn espied the place he halted with an exclamation of profound astonishment.

"By all my ancestors!" he ejaculated. "That I should have lived to witness the reality of the fabled Carrion Caves! If these indeed be they we have found a way beyond the ice-barrier.

"The ancient chronicles of the first historians of Barsoom —so ancient that we have for ages considered them mythology—record the passing of the yellow men from the ravages of the green hordes that overran Barsoom as the drying up of the great oceans drove the dominant races from their strongholds.

"They tell of the wanderings of the remnants of this once powerful race, harassed at every step, until at last they found a way through the ice-barrier of the north to a fertile valley at the pole.

"At the opening to the subterranean passage that led to their haven of refuge a mighty battle was fought in which the yellow men were victorious, and within the caves that gave ingress to their new home they piled the bodies of the dead, both yellow and green, that the stench might warn away their enemies from further pursuit.

"And ever since that long-gone day have the dead of this fabled land been carried to the Carrion Caves, that in death and decay they might serve their country and warn away invading enemies. Here, too, is brought, so the fable runs, all the waste stuff of the nation—everything that is subject to rot, and that can add to the foul stench that assails our nostrils.

"And death lurks at every step among rotting dead, for here the fierce apts lair, adding to the putrid accumulation with the fragments of their own prey which they cannot devour. It is a horrid avenue to our goal, but it is the only one."

"You are sure, then, that we have found the way to the land of the yellow men?" I cried.

"As sure as may be," he replied; "having only ancient legend to support my belief. But see how closely, so far, each detail tallies with the world-old story of the hegira of the yellow race. Yes, I am sure that we have discovered the way to their ancient hiding place."

"If it be true, and let us pray that such may be the case," I said, "then here may we solve the mystery of the disappearance of Tardos Mors, Jeddak of Helium, and Mors Kajak, his son, for no other spot upon Barsoom has remained unexplored by the many expeditions and the countless spies that have been searching for them for nearly two years. The last word that came from them was that they sought Carthoris, my own brave son, beyond the ice-barrier."

As we talked we had been approaching the entrance to the cave, and as we crossed the threshold I ceased to wonder that the ancient green enemies of the yellow men had been halted by the horrors of that awful way.

The bones of dead men lay man high upon the broad floor of the first cave, and over all was a putrid mush of decaying flesh, through which the apts had beaten a hideous trail toward the entrance to the second cave beyond.

The roof of this first apartment was low, like all that we traversed subsequently, so that the foul odors were confined and condensed to such an extent that they seemed to possess tangible substance. One was almost tempted to draw his short-sword and hew his way through in search of pure air beyond.

"Can man breathe this polluted air and live?" asked Thuvan Dihn, choking.

"Not for long, I imagine," I replied; "so let us make haste. I will go first, and you bring up the rear, with Woola between. Come," and with the words I dashed forward, across the fetid mass of putrefaction.

It was not until we had passed through seven caves of different sizes and varying but little in the power and quality of their stenches that we met with any physical opposition. Then, within the eighth cave, we came upon a lair of apts.

A full score of the mighty beasts were disposed about the chamber. Some were sleeping, while others tore at the fresh-killed carcasses of new-brought prey, or fought among themselves in their love-making.

Here in the dim light of their subterranean home the value of their great eyes was apparent, for these inner caves are shrouded in perpetual gloom that is but little less than utter darkness.

To attempt to pass through the midst of that fierce herd seemed, even to me, the height of folly, and so I proposed to Thuvan Dihn that he return to the outer world with Woola, that the two might find their way to civilization and come again with a sufficient force to overcome not only the apts, but any further obstacles that might lie between us and our goal.

"In the meantime," I continued, "I may discover some means of winning my way alone to the land of the yellow men, but if I am unsuccessful one life only will have been sacrificed. Should we all go on and perish, there will be none to guide a succoring party to Dejah Thoris and your daughter."

"I shall not return and leave you here alone, John Carter," replied Thuvan Dihn. "Whether you go on to victory or death, the Jeddak of Ptarth remains at your side. I have spoken."

I knew from his tone that it were useless to attempt to argue the question, and so I compromised by sending Woola back with a hastily penned note enclosed in a small metal case and fastened about his neck. I commanded the faithful creature to seek Carthoris at Helium, and though half a world and countless dangers lay between I knew that if the thing could be done Woola would do it.

Equipped as he was by nature with marvelous speed and endurance, and with frightful ferocity that made him a match for any single enemy of the way, his keen intelligence and wondrous instinct should easily furnish all else that was needed for the successful accomplishment of his mission.

It was with evident reluctance that the great beast turned to leave me in compliance with my command, and ere he had gone I could not resist the inclination to throw my arms about his great neck in a parting hug. He rubbed his cheek against mine in a final caress, and a moment later was speeding through the Carrion Caves toward the outer world.

In my note to Carthoris I had given explicit directions for locating the Carrion Caves, impressing upon him the necessity for making entrance to the country beyond through this avenue, and not to attempt under any circumstances to cross the ice-barrier with a fleet. I told him that what lay beyond the eighth cave I could not even guess; but I was sure that somewhere upon the other side of the ice-barrier his mother lay in the power of Matai Shang, and that possibly his grandfather and great-grandfather as well, if they lived.

Further, I advised him to call upon Kulan Tith and the son of Thuvan Dihn for warriors and ships that the expedition might be sufficiently strong to insure success at the first blow.

"And," I concluded, "if there be time bring Tars Tarkas with you, for if I live until you reach me I can think of few greater pleasures than to fight once more, shoulder to shoulder, with my old friend."

When Woola had left us Thuvan Dihn and I, hiding in the seventh cave, discussed and discarded many plans for crossing the eighth chamber. From where we stood we saw that the fighting among the apts was growing less, and that many that had been feeding had ceased and lain down to sleep.

Presently it became apparent that in a short time all the ferocious monsters might be peacefully slumbering, and thus a hazardous opportunity be presented to us to cross through their lair.

One by one the remaining brutes stretched themselves upon the bubbling decomposition that covered the mass of

84

bones upon the floor of their den, until but a single apt remained awake. This huge fellow roamed restlessly about, nosing among his companions and the abhorrent litter of the cave.

Occasionally he would stop to peer intently toward first one of the exits from the chamber and then the other. His whole demeanor was as of one who acts as sentry.

We were at last forced to the belief that he would not sleep while the other occupants of the lair slept, and so cast about in our minds for some scheme whereby we might trick him. Finally I suggested a plan to Thuvan Dihn, and as it seemed as good as any that we had discussed we decided to put it to the test.

To this end Thuvan Dihn placed himself close against the cave's wall, beside the entrance to the eighth chamber, while I deliberately showed myself to the guardian apt as he looked toward our retreat. Then I sprang to the opposite side of the entrance, flattening my body close to the wall.

Without a sound the great beast moved rapidly toward the seventh cave to see what manner of intruder had thus rashly penetrated so far within the precincts of his habitation.

As he poked his head through the narrow aperture that connects the two caves a heavy long-sword was awaiting him upon either hand, and before he had an opportunity to emit even a single growl his severed head rolled at our feet.

Quickly we glanced into the eighth chamber—not an apt had moved. Crawling over the carcass of the huge beast that blocked the doorway Thuvan Dihn and I cautiously entered the forbidding and dangerous den.

Like snails we wound our silent and careful way among the huge, recumbent forms. The only sound above our breathing was the sucking noise of our feet as we lifted them from the ooze of decaying flesh through which we crept.

Halfway across the chamber and one of the mighty beasts directly before me moved restlessly at the very instant that my foot was poised above his head, over which I must step. Breathlessly I waited, balancing upon one foot, for I did not dare move a muscle. In my right hand was my keen short-sword, the point hovering an inch above the thick fur beneath which beat the savage heart.

Finally the apt relaxed, sighing, as with the passing of a bad dream, and resumed the regular respiration of deep slumber. I planted my raised foot beyond the fierce head and an instant later had stepped over the beast.

Thuvan Dihn followed directly after me, and another moment found us at the further door, undetected.

The Carrion Caves consist of a series of twenty-seven connecting chambers, and present the appearance of having been eroded by running water in some far-gone age when a mighty river found its way to the south through this single breach in the barrier of rock and ice that hems the country of the pole.

Thuvan Dihn and I traversed the remaining nineteen caverns without adventure or mishap.

We were afterward to learn that but once a month is it possible to find all the apts of the Carrion Caves in a single chamber.

At other times they roam singly or in pairs in and out of the caves, so that it would have been practically impossible for two men to have passed through the entire twenty-seven chambers without encountering an apt in nearly every one of them. Once a month they sleep for a full day, and it was our good fortune to stumble by accident upon one of these occasions.

Beyond the last cave we emerged into a desolate country of snow and ice, but found a well-marked trail leading north. The way was boulder-strewn, as had been that south of the barrier, so that we could see but a short distance ahead of us at any time.

After a couple of hours we passed round a huge boulder to come to a steep declivity leading down into a valley.

Directly before us we saw a half dozen men—fierce, black-bearded fellows, with skins the color of a ripe lemon.

"The yellow men of Barsoom!" ejaculated Thuvan Dihn, as though even now that he saw them he found it scarce possible to believe that the very race we expected to find hidden in this remote and inaccessible land did really exist.

We withdrew behind an adjacent boulder to watch the actions of the little party, which stood huddled at the foot of another huge rock, their backs toward us.

One of them was peering round the edge of the granite mass as though watching one who approached from the opposite side.

Presently the object of his scrutiny came within the range

of my vision and I saw that it was another yellow man. All were clothed in magnificent furs—the six in the black and yellow striped hide of the orluk, while he who approached alone was resplendent in the pure white skin of an apt.

The yellow men were armed with two swords, and a short javelin was slung across the back of each, while from their left arms hung cuplike shields no larger than a dinner plate, the concave sides of which turned outward toward an antagonist.

They seemed puny and futile implements of safety against an even ordinary swordsman, but I was later to see the purpose of them and with what wondrous dexterity the yellow men manipulate them.

One of the swords which each of the warriors carried caught my immediate attention. I call it a sword, but really it was a sharp-edged blade with a complete hook at the far end.

The other sword was of about the same length as the hooked instrument, and somewhere between that of my long-sword and my short-sword. It was straight and two-edged. In addition to the weapons I have innumerated each man carried a dagger in his harness.

As the white-furred one approached, the six grasped their swords more firmly—the hooked instrument in the left hand, the straight sword in the right, while above the left wrist the small shield was held rigid upon a metal bracelet.

As the lone warrior came opposite them the six rushed out upon him with fiendish yells that resembled nothing more closely than the savage war cry of the Apaches of the South-west.

Instantly the attacked drew both his swords, and as the six fell upon him I witnessed as pretty fighting as one might care to see.

With their sharp hooks the combatants attempted to take hold of an adversary, but like lightning the cupshaped shield would spring before the darting weapon and into its hollow the hook would plunge.

Once the lone warrior caught an antagonist in the side with his hook, and drawing him close ran his sword through him.

But the odds were too unequal, and, though he who fought alone was by far the best and bravest of them all, I saw that it was but a question of time before the remaining five would find an opening through his marvelous guard and bring him down.

Now my sympathies have ever been with the weaker side of an argument, and though I knew nothing of the cause of the trouble I could not stand idly by and see a brave man butchered by superior numbers.

As a matter of fact I presume I gave little attention to seeking an excuse, for I love a good fight too well to need any other reason for joining in when one is afoot.

So it was that before Thuvan Dihn knew what I was about he saw me standing by the side of the white-clad yellow man, battling like mad with his five adversaries.

… social manipulation about.

Now my sympathies have ever been with the [worker side?] of an argument, and though I know nothing of the cause of the trouble, I … … … … … … brave man

WITH THE YELLOW MEN

THUVAN DIHN was not long in joining me; and, though we found the hooked weapon a strange and savage thing with which to deal, the three of us soon despatched the five black-bearded warriors who opposed us.

When the battle was over our new acquaintance turned to me, and removing the shield from his wrist, held it out. I did not know the significance of his act, but judged that it was but a form of expressing his gratitude to me.

I afterward learned that it symbolized the offering of a man's life in return for some great favor done him; and my act of refusing, which I had immediately done, was what was expected of me.

"Then accept from Talu, Prince of Marentina," said the yellow man, "this token of my gratitude," and reaching beneath one of his wide sleeves he withdrew a bracelet and placed it upon my arm. He then went through the same ceremony with Thuvan Dihn.

Next he asked our names, and from what land we hailed. He seemed quite familiar with the geography of the outerworld, and when I said I was from Helium he raised his brows.

"Ah," he said, "you seek your ruler and his company?"

"Know you of them?" I asked.

"But little more than that they were captured by my uncle, Salensus Oll, Jeddak of Jeddaks, Ruler of Okar, land of the yellow men of Barsoom. As to their fate I know nothing, for I am at war with my uncle, who would crush my power in the principality of Marentina.

"These from whom you have just saved me are warriors he has sent out to find and slay me, for they know that often I come alone to hunt and kill the sacred apt which Salensus Oll so much reveres. It is partly because I hate his religion that Salensus Oll hates me; but mostly does he fear my growing power and the great faction which has arisen throughout

89

Okar that would be glad to see me ruler of Okar and Jeddak of Jeddaks in his place.

"He is a cruel and tyrannous master whom all hate, and were it not for the great fear they have of him I could raise an army overnight that would wipe out the few that might remain loyal to him. My own people are faithful to me, and the little valley of Marentina has paid no tribute to the court of Salensus Oll for a year.

"Nor can he force us, for a dozen men may hold the narrow way to Marentina against a million. But now, as to thine own affairs. How may I aid you? My palace is at your disposal, if you wish to honor me by coming to Marentina."

"When our work is done we shall be glad to accept your invitation," I replied. "But now you can assist us most by directing us to the court of Salensus Oll, and suggesting some means by which we may gain admission to the city and the palace, or whatever other place we find our friends to be confined."

Talu gazed ruefully at our smooth faces and at Thuvan Dihn's red skin and my white one.

"First you must come to Marentina," he said, "for a great change must be wrought in your appearance before you can hope to enter any city in Okar. You must have yellow faces and black beards, and your apparel and trappings must be those least likely to arouse suspicion. In my palace is one who can make you appear as truly yellow men as does Salensus Oll himself."

His counsel seemed wise; and as there was apparently no other way to insure a successful entry to Kadabra, the capital city of Okar, we set out with Talu, Prince of Marentina, for his little, rock-bound country.

The way was over some of the worst traveling I have ever seen, and I do not wonder that in this land where there are neither thoats nor fliers that Marentina is in little fear of invasion; but at last we reached our destination, the first view of which I had from a slight elevation a half-mile from the city.

Nestled in a deep valley lay a city of Martian concrete, whose every street and plaza and open space was roofed with glass. All about lay snow and ice, but there was none upon the rounded, domelike, crystal covering that enveloped the whole city.

Then I saw how these people combatted the rigors of the arctic, and lived in luxury and comfort in the midst of a land of perpetual ice. Their cities were veritable hothouses, and when I had come within this one my respect and admiration for the scientific and engineering skill of this buried nation was unbounded.

The moment we entered the city Talu threw off his outer garments of fur, as did we, and I saw that his apparel differed but little from that of the red races of Barsoom. Except for his leathern harness, covered thick with jewels and metal, he was naked, nor could one have comfortably worn apparel in that warm and humid atmosphere.

For three days we remained the guests of Prince Talu, and during that time he showered upon us every attention and courtesy within his power. He showed us all that was of interest in his great city.

The Marentina atmosphere plant will maintain life indefinitely in the cities of the north pole after all life upon the balance of dying Mars is extinct through the failure of the air supply, should the great central plant again cease functioning as it did upon that memorable occasion that gave me the opportunity of restoring life and happiness to the strange world that I had already learned to love so well.

He showed us the heating system that stores the sun's rays in great reservoirs beneath the city, and how little is necessary to maintain the perpetual summer heat of the glorious garden spot within this arctic paradise.

Broad avenues of sod sewn with the seed of the ocher vegetation of the dead sea bottoms carried the noiseless traffic of light and airy ground fliers that are the only form of artificial transportation used north of the gigantic ice-barrier.

The broad tires of these unique fliers are but rubber-like gas bags filled with the eighth Barsoomian ray, or ray of propulsion—that remarkable discovery of the Martians that has made possible the great fleets of mighty airships that render the red man of the outer world supreme. It is this ray which propels the inherent or reflected light of the planet off into space, and when confined gives to the Martian craft their airy buoyancy.

The ground fliers of Marentina contain just sufficient buoyancy in their automobile-like wheels to give the cars traction for steering purposes; and though the hind wheels are geared to the engine, and aid in driving the machine, the bulk of this work is carried by a small propeller at the stern.

I know of no more delightful sensation than that of riding in one of these luxuriously appointed cars which skim, light and airy as feathers, along the soft, mossy avenues of Marentina. They move with absolute noiselessness between borders of crimson sward and beneath arching trees gorgeous with the wondrous blooms that mark so many of the highly cultivated varieties of Barsoomian vegetation.

By the end of the third day the court barber—I can think of no other earthly appellation by which to describe him—had wrought so remarkable a transformation in both Thuvan Dihn and myself that our own wives would never have known us. Our skins were of the same lemon color as his own, and great, black beards and mustaches had been deftly affixed to our smooth faces. The trappings of warriors of Okar aided in the deception; and for wear beyond the hothouse cities we each had suits of the black- and yellow-striped orluk.

Talu gave us careful directions for the journey to Kadabra, the capital city of the Okar nation, which is the racial name of the yellow men. This good friend even accompanied us part way, and then, promising to aid us in any way that he found possible, bade us adieu.

On parting he slipped upon my finger a curiously wrought ring set with a dead-black, lusterless stone, which appeared more like a bit of bituminous coal than the priceless Barsoomian gem which in reality it is.

"There had been but three others cut from the mother stone," he said, "which is in my possession. These three are worn by nobles high in my confidence, all of whom have been sent on secret missions to the court of Salensus Oll.

"Should you come within fifty feet of any of these three you will feel a rapid, pricking sensation in the finger upon which you wear this ring. He who wears one of its mates will experience the same feeling; it is caused by an electrical action that takes place the moment two of these gems cut from the same mother stone come within the radius of each other's power. By it you will know that a friend is at hand upon whom you may depend for assistance in time of need.

"Should another wearer of one of these gems call upon you for aid do not deny him, and should death threaten you swallow the ring rather than let it fall into the hands of enemies. Guard it with your life, John Carter, for some day it may mean more than life to you."

With this parting admonition our good friend turned back toward Marentina, and we set our faces in the direction of the city of Kadabra and the court of Salensus Oll, Jeddak of Jeddaks.

That very evening we came within sight of the walled and glass-roofed city of Kadabra. It lies in a low depression near the pole, surrounded by rocky, snow-clad hills. From the pass through which we entered the valley we had a splendid view of this great city of the north. Its crystal domes sparkled in the brilliant sunlight gleaming above the frost-covered outer wall that circles the entire one hundred miles of its circumference.

At regular intervals great gates give entrance to the city; but even at the distance from which we looked upon the massive pile we could see that all were closed, and, in accordance with Talu's suggestion, we deferred attempting to enter the city until the following morning.

As he had said, we found numerous caves in the hillsides about us, and into one of these we crept for the night. Our warm orluk skins kept us perfectly comfortable, and it was only after a most refreshing sleep that we awoke shortly after daylight on the following morning.

Already the city was astir, and from several of the gates we saw parties of yellow men emerging. Following closely each detail of the instructions given us by our good friend of Marentina, we remained concealed for several hours until one party of some half dozen warriors had passed along the trail below our hiding place and entered the hills by way of the pass along which we had come the previous evening.

After giving them time to get well out of sight of our cave, Thuvan Dihn and I crept out and followed them, overtaking them when they were well into the hills.

When we had come almost to them I called aloud to their leader, when the whole party halted and turned toward us.

The crucial test had come. Could we but deceive these men the rest would be comparatively easy.

"Kaor!" I cried as I came closer to them.

"Kaor!" responded the officer in charge of the party.

"We be from Illall," I continued, giving the name of the most remote city of Okar, which has little or no intercourse with Kadabra. "Only yesterday we arrived, and this morning the captain of the gate told us that you were setting out to hunt orluks, which is a sport we do not find in our own neighborhood. We have hastened after you to pray that you allow us to accompany you."

The officer was entirely deceived, and graciously permitted us to go with them for the day. The chance guess that they were bound upon an orluk hunt proved correct, and Talu had said that the chances were ten to one that such would be the mission of any party leaving Kadabra by the pass through which we entered the valley, since that way leads directly to the vast plains frequented by this elephantine beast of prey.

In so far as the hunt was concerned, the day was a failure, for we did not see a single orluk; but this proved more than fortunate for us, since the yellow men were so chagrined by their misfortune that they would not enter the city by the same gate by which they had left it in the morning, as it seemed that they had made great boasts to the captain of that gate about their skill at this dangerous sport.

We, therefore, approached Kadabra at a point several miles from that at which the party had quitted it in the morning, and so were relieved of the danger of embarrassing questions and explanations on the part of the gate captain, whom we had said had directed us to this particular hunting party.

We had come quite close to the city when my attention was attracted toward a tall, black shaft that reared its head several hundred feet into the air from what appeared to be a tangled mass of junk or wreckage, now partially snow-covered.

I did not dare venture an inquiry for fear of arousing suspicion by evident ignorance of something which as a yellow man I should have known; but before we reached the city gate I was to learn the purpose of that grim shaft and the meaning of the mighty accumulation beneath it.

We had come almost to the gate when one of the party called to his fellows, at the same time pointing toward the distant southern horizon. Following the direction he indicated, my eyes descried the hull of a large flier approaching rapidly from above the crest of the encircling hills.

"Still other fools who would solve the mysteries of the forbidden north," said the officer, half to himself. "Will they never cease their fatal curiosity?"

"Let us hope not," answered one of the warriors, "for then what should we do for slaves and sport?"

"True; but what stupid beasts they are to continue to come to a region from whence none of them ever has returned."

"Let us tarry and watch the end of this one," suggested one of the men.

The officer looked toward the city.

"The watch has seen him," he said; "we may remain, for we may be needed."

I looked toward the city and saw several hundred warriors issuing from the nearest gate. They moved leisurely, as though there were no need for haste—nor was there, as I was presently to learn.

Then I turned my eyes once more toward the flier. She was moving rapidly toward the city, and when she had come close enough I was surprised to see that her propellers were idle.

Straight for that grim shaft she bore. At the last minute I saw the great blades move to reverse her, yet on she came as though drawn by some mighty, irresistible power.

Intense excitement prevailed upon her deck, where men were running hither and thither, manning the guns and preparing to launch the small, one-man fliers, a fleet of which is part of the equipment of every Martian war vessel. Closer and closer to the black shaft the ship sped. In another instant she must strike, and then I saw the familiar signal flown that sends the lesser boats in a great flock from the deck of the mother ship.

Instantly a hundred tiny fliers rose from her deck, like a swarm of huge dragon flies; but scarcely were they clear of the battleship than the nose of each turned toward the shaft, and they, too, rushed on at frightful speed toward the same now seemingly inevitable end that menaced the larger vessel.

A moment later the collision came. Men were hurled in every direction from the ship's deck, while she, bent and crumpled, took the last, long plunge to the scrap-heap at the shaft's base.

With her fell a shower of her own tiny fliers, for each of them had come in violent collision with the solid shaft.

I noticed that the wrecked fliers scraped down the shaft's side, and that their fall was not as rapid as might have been expected; and then suddenly the secret of the shaft burst upon me, and with it an explanation of the cause that prevented a flier that passed too far across the ice-barrier ever returning.

The shaft was a mighty magnet, and when once a vessel came within the radius of its powerful attraction for the aluminum steel that enters so largely into the construction of all Barsoomian craft, no power on earth could prevent such an end as we had just witnessed.

I afterward learned that the shaft rests directly over the magnetic pole of Mars, but whether this adds in any way to its incalculable power of attraction I do not know. I am a fighting man, not a scientist.

Here, at last, was an explanation of the long absence of Tardos Mors and Mors Kajak. These valiant and intrepid warriors had dared the mysteries and dangers of the frozen north to search for Carthoris, whose long absence had bowed in grief the head of his beautiful mother, Dejah Thoris, Princess of Helium.

The moment that the last of the fliers came to rest at the base of the shaft the black-bearded, yellow warriors swarmed over the mass of wreckage upon which they lay, making prisoners of those who were uninjured and occasionally despatching with a sword-thrust one of the wounded who seemed prone to resent their taunts and insults.

A few of the uninjured red men battled bravely against their cruel foes, but for the most part they seemed too overwhelmed by the horror of the catastrophe that had befallen them to do more than submit supinely to the golden chains with which they were menacled.

When the last of the prisoners had been confined, the party returned to the city, at the gate of which we met a pack of fierce, gold-collared apts, each of which marched between two warriors, who held them with strong chains of the same metal as their collars.

Just beyond the gate the attendants loosened the whole

terrible herd, and as they bounded off toward the grim, black shaft I did not need to ask to know their mission. Had there not been those within the cruel city of Kadabra who needed succor far worse than the poor unfortunate dead and dying out there in the cold upon the bent and broken carcasses of a thousand fliers I could not have restrained my desire to hasten back and do battle with those horrid creatures that had been despatched to rend and devour them.

As it was I could but follow the yellow warriors, with bowed head, and give thanks for the chance that had given Thuvan Dihn and me such easy ingress to the capital of Salensus Oll.

Once within the gates, we had no difficulty in eluding our friends of the morning, and presently found ourselves in a Martian hostelry.

IN DURANCE

THE public houses of Barsoom, I have found, vary but little. There is no privacy for other than married couples.

Men without their wives are escorted to a large chamber, the floor of which is usually of white marble or heavy glass, kept scrupulously clean. Here are many small, raised platforms for the guest's sleeping silks and furs, and if he have none of his own clean, fresh ones are furnished at a nominal charge.

Once a man's belongings have been deposited upon one of these platforms he is a guest of the house, and that platform his own until he leaves. No one will disturb or molest his belongings, as there are no thieves upon Mars.

As assassination is the one thing to be feared, the proprietors of the hostelries furnish armed guards, who pace back and forth through the sleeping-rooms day and night. The number of guards and gorgeousness of their trappings quite usually denote the status of the hotel.

No meals are served in these houses, but generally a public eating place adjoins them. Baths are connected with the sleeping chambers, and each guest is required to bathe daily or depart from the hotel.

Usually on a second or third floor there is a large sleeping-room for single women guests, but its appointments do not vary materially from the chamber occupied by men. The guards who watch the women remain in the corridor outside the sleeping chamber, while female slaves pace back and forth among the sleepers within, ready to notify the warriors should their presence be required.

I was surprised to note that all the guards with the hotel at which we stopped were red men, and on inquiring of one of them I learned that they were slaves purchased by the proprietors of the hotels from the government. The man whose post was past my sleeping platform had been commander of the navy of a great Martian nation; but fate had carried his flagship across the ice-barrier within the radius of power of the magnetic shaft, and now for many tedious years he had been a slave of the yellow men.

He told me that princes, jeds, and even jeddaks of the outer world, were among the menials who served the yellow race; but when I asked him if he had heard of the fate of Mors Kajak or Tardos Mors he shook his head, saying that he never had heard of their being prisoners here, though he was very familiar with the reputations and fame they bore in the outer world.

Neither had he heard any rumor of the coming of the Father of Therns and the black dator of the First Born, but he hastened to explain that he knew little of what took place within the palace. I could see that he wondered not a little that a yellow man should be so inquisitive about certain red prisoners from beyond the ice-barrier, and that I should be so ignorant of customs and conditions among my own race.

In fact, I had forgotten my disguise upon discovering a red man pacing before my sleeping platform; but his growing expression of surprise warned me in time, for I had no mind to reveal my identity to any unless some good could come of it, and I did not see how this poor fellow could serve me yet, though I had it in my mind that later I might be the means of serving him and all the other thousands of prisoners who do the bidding of their stern masters in Kadabra.

Thuvan Dihn and I discussed our plans as we sat together among our sleeping silks and furs that night in the midst of the hundreds of yellow men who occupied the apartment with us. We spoke in low whispers, but, as that is only what courtesy demands in a public sleeping place, we roused no suspicion.

At last, determining that all must be but idle speculation until after we had had a chance to explore the city and attempt to put into execution the plan Talu had suggested, we bade each other good night and turned to sleep.

After breakfasting the following morning we set out to see Kadabra, and as, through the generosity of the prince of Marentina, we were well supplied with the funds current in Okar we purchased a handsome ground flier. Having learned to drive them while in Marentina, we spent a delightful and profitable day exploring the city, and late in the afternoon at the hour Talu told us we would find government officials in their offices we stopped before a magnificent building on the plaza opposite the royal grounds and the palace.

Here we walked boldly in past the armed guard at the door, to be met by a red slave within who asked our wishes.

"Tell Sorav, your master, that two warriors from Illall wish to take service in the palace guard," I said.

Sorav, Talu had told us, was the commander of the forces of the palace, and as men from the further cities of Okar—and especially Illall—were less likely to be tainted with the germ of intrigue which had for years infected the household of Salensus Oll, he was sure that we would be welcomed and few questions asked us.

He had primed us with such general information as he thought would be necessary for us to pass muster before Sorav, after which we would have to undergo a further examination before Salensus Oll that he might determine our physical fitness and our ability as warriors.

The little experience we had had with the strange hooked sword of the yellow man and his cuplike shield made it seem rather unlikely that either of us could pass this final test, but there was the chance that we might be quartered in the palace of Salensus Oll for several days after being accepted by Sorav before the Jeddak of Jeddaks would find time to put us to the final test.

After a wait of several minutes in an ante-chamber we were summoned into the private office of Sorav, where we were courteously greeted by this ferocious-appearing, black-bearded officer. He asked us our names and stations in our own city, and having received replies that were evidently satisfactory to him, he put certain questions to us that Talu had foreseen and prepared us for.

The interview could not have lasted over ten minutes when Sorav summoned an aid whom he instructed to record us properly, and then escort us to the quarters in the palace which are set aside for aspirants to membership in the palace guard.

The aid took us to his own office first, where he measured and weighed and photographed us simultaneously with a machine ingeniously devised for that purpose, five copies being instantly reproduced in five different offices of the government, two of which are located in other cities miles distant. Then he led us through the palace grounds to the main guardroom of the palace, there turning us over to the officer in charge.

This individual again questioned us briefly, and finally despatched a soldier to guide us to our quarters. These we found located upon the second floor of the palace in a semidetached tower at the rear of the edifice.

When we asked our guide why we were quartered so far from the guardroom he replied that the custom of the older members of the guard of picking quarrels with aspirants to try their metal had resulted in so many deaths that it was found difficult to maintain the guard at its full strength while this custom prevailed. Salensus Oll had, therefore, set apart these quarters for aspirants, and here they were securely locked against the danger of attack by members of the guard.

This unwelcome information put a sudden check to all our well-laid plans, for it meant that we should virtually be prisoners in the palace of Salensus Oll until the time that he should see fit to give us the final examination for efficiency.

As it was this interval upon which we had banked to accomplish so much in our search for Dejah Thoris and Thuvia of Ptarth, our chagrin was unbounded when we heard the great lock click behind our guide as he had quitted us after ushering us into the chambers we were to occupy.

With a wry face I turned to Thuvan Dihn. My companion but shook his head disconsolately and walked to one of the windows upon the far side of the apartment.

Scarcely had he gazed beyond them than he called to me in a tone of suppressed excitement and surprise. In an instant I was by his side.

"Look!" said Thuvan Dihn, pointing toward the courtyard below.

As my eyes followed the direction indicated I saw two women pacing back and forth in an enclosed garden.

At the same moment I recognized them—they were Dejah Thoris and Thuvia of Ptarth!

There were they whom I had trailed from one pole to another, the length of a world. Only ten feet of space and a few metal bars separated me from them.

With a cry I attracted their attention, and as Dejah Thoris looked up full into my eyes I made the sign of love that the men of Barsoom make to their women.

101

To my astonishment and horror her head went high, and as a look of utter contempt touched her finely chiseled features she turned her back full upon me. My body is covered with the scars of a thousand conflicts, but never in all my long life have I suffered such anguish from a wound, for this time the steel of a woman's look had entered my heart.

With a groan I turned away and buried my face in my arms. I heard Thuvan Dihn call aloud to Thuvia, but an instant later his exclamation of surprise betokened that he, too, had been repulsed by his own daughter.

"They will not even listen," he cried to me. "They have put their hands over their ears and walked to the farther end of the garden. Ever heard you of such mad work, John Carter? The two must be bewitched."

Presently I mustered the courage to return to the window, for even though she spurned me I loved her, and could not keep my eyes from feasting upon her divine face and figure, but when she saw me looking she again turned away.

I was at my wit's end to account for her strange actions, and that Thuvia, too, had turned against her father seemed incredible. Could it be that my incomparable princess still clung to the hideous faith from which I had rescued her world? Could it be that she looked upon me with loathing and contempt because I had returned from the Valley Dor, or because I had desecrated the temples and persons of the Holy Therns?

To naught else could I ascribe her strange deportment, yet it seemed far from possible that such could be the case, for the love of Dejah Thoris for John Carter had been a great and wondrous love—far above racial distinctions, creed, or religion.

As I gazed ruefully at the back of her haughty, royal head a gate at the opposite end of the garden opened and a man entered. As he did so he turned and slipped something into the hand of the yellow guardsman beyond the gate, nor was the distance too great that I might not see that money had passed between them.

Instantly I knew that this newcomer had bribed his way within the garden. Then he turned in the direction of the two women, and I saw that he was none other than Thurid, the black dator of the First Born.

He approached quite close to them before he spoke, and as they turned at the sound of his voice I saw Dejah Thoris shrink from him.

There was a nasty leer upon his face as he stepped close to her and spoke again. I could not hear his words, but her answer came clearly.

"The granddaughter of Tardos Mors can always die," she said, "but she could never live at the price you name."

Then I saw the black scoundrel go upon his knees beside her, fairly groveling in the dirt, pleading with her. Only part of what he said came to me, for though he was evidently laboring under the stress of passion and excitement, it was equally apparent that he did not dare raise his voice for fear of detection.

"I would save you from Matai Shang," I heard him say. "You know the fate that awaits you at his hands. Would you not choose me rather than the other?"

"I would choose neither," replied Dejah Thoris, "even were I free to choose, as you know well I am not."

"You *are* free!" he cried. "John Carter, Prince of Helium, is dead."

"I know better than that; but even were he dead, and I must needs choose another mate, it should be a plant man or a great white ape in preference to either Matai Shang or you, black calot," she answered with a sneer of contempt.

Of a sudden the vicious beast lost all control of himself, as with a vile oath he leaped at the slender woman, gripping her tender throat in his brute clutch. Thuvia screamed and sprang to aid her fellow-prisoner, and at the same instant I, too, went mad, and tearing at the bars that spanned my window I ripped them from their sockets as they had been but copper wire.

Hurling myself through the aperture I reached the garden, but a hundred feet from where the black was choking the life from my Dejah Thoris, and with a single great bound I was upon him. I spoke no word as I tore his defiling fingers from that beautiful throat, nor did I utter a sound as I hurled him twenty feet from me.

Foaming with rage, Thurid regained his feet and charged me like a mad bull.

"Yellow man," he shrieked, "you knew not upon whom you had laid your vile hands, but ere I am done with you,

you will know well what it means to offend the person of a First Born."

Then he was upon me, reaching for my throat, and precisely as I had done that day in the courtyard of the Temple of Issus I did here in the garden of the palace of Salensus Oll. I ducked beneath his outstretched arms, and as he lunged past me I planted a terrific right upon the side of his jaw.

Just as he had done upon that other occasion he did now. Like a top he spun round, his knees gave beneath him, and he crumpled to the ground at my feet. Then I heard a voice behind me.

It was the deep voice of authority that marks the ruler of men, and when I turned to face the resplendent figure of a giant yellow man I did not need to ask to know that it was Salensus Oll. At his right stood Matai Shang, and behind them a score of guardsmen.

"Who are you," he cried, "and what means this intrusion within the precincts of the women's garden? I do not recall your face. How came you here?"

But for his last words I should have forgotten my disguise entirely and told him outright that I was John Carter, Prince of Helium; but his question recalled me to myself. I pointed to the dislodged bars of the window above.

"I am an aspirant to membership in the palace guard," I said, "and from yonder window in the tower where I was confined awaiting the final test for fitness I saw this brute attack the—this woman. I could not stand idly by, O Jeddak, and see this thing done within the very palace grounds, and yet feel that I was fit to serve and guard your royal person."

I had evidently made an impression upon the ruler of Okar by my fair words, and when he had turned to Dejah Thoris and Thuvia of Ptarth, and both had corroborated my statements it began to look pretty dark for Thurid.

I saw the ugly gleam in Matai Shang's evil eyes as Dejah Thoris narrated all that had passed between Thurid and herself, and when she came to that part which dealt with my interference with the dator of the First Born her gratitude was quite apparent, though I could see by her eyes that something puzzled her strangely.

I did not wonder at her attitude toward me while others

were present; but that she should have denied me while she and Thuvia were the only occupants of the garden still cut me sorely.

As the examination proceeded I cast a glance at Thurid and startled him looking wide-eyed and wonderingly at me, and then of a sudden he laughed full in my face.

A moment later Salensus Oll turned toward the black.

"What have you to say in explanation of these charges?" he asked in a deep and terrible voice. "Dare you aspire to one whom the Father of Therns has chosen—one who might even be a fit mate for the Jeddak of Jeddaks himself?"

And then the black-bearded tyrant turned and cast a sudden greedy look upon Dejah Thoris, as though with the words a new thought and a new desire had sprung up within his mind and breast.

Thurid had been about to reply and, with a malicious grin upon his face, was pointing an accusing finger at me, when Salensus Oll's words and the expression of his face cut him short.

A cunning look crept into his eyes, and I knew from the expression of his face that his next words were not the ones he had intended to speak.

"O Mightiest of Jeddaks," he said, "the man and the women do not speak the truth. The fellow had come into the garden to assist them to escape. I was beyond and overheard their conversation, and when I entered, the woman screamed and the man sprang upon me and would have killed me.

"What know you of this man? He is a stranger to you, and I dare say that you will find him an enemy and a spy. Let him be put on trial, Salensus Oll, rather than your friend and guest, Thurid, Dator of the First Born."

Salensus Oll looked puzzled. He turned again and looked upon Dejah Thoris, and then Thurid stepped quite close to him and whispered something in his ear—what, I know not.

Presently the yellow ruler turned to one of his officers.

"See that this man be securely confined until we have time to go deeper into this affair," he commanded, "and as bars alone seem inadequate to restrain him, let chains be added."

Then he turned and left the garden, taking Dejah Thoris with him—his hand upon her shoulder. Thurid and Matai

Shang went also, and as they reached the gateway the black turned and laughed again aloud in my face.

What could be the meaning of his sudden change toward me? Could he suspect my true identity? It must be that, and the thing that had betrayed me was the trick and blow that had laid him low for the second time.

As the guards dragged me away my heart was very sad and bitter indeed, for now to the two relentless enemies that had hounded her for so long another and a more powerful one had been added, for I would have been but a fool had I not recognized the sudden love for Dejah Thoris that had just been born in the terrible breast of Salensus Oll, Jeddak of Jeddaks, ruler of Okar.

THE PIT OF PLENTY

I DID not languish long within the prison of Salensus Oll. During the short time that I lay there, fettered with chains of gold, I often wondered as to the fate of Thuvan Dihn, Jeddak of Ptarth.

My brave companion had followed me into the garden as I attacked Thurid, and when Salensus Oll had left with Dejah Thoris and the others, leaving Thuvia of Ptarth behind, he, too, had remained in the garden with his daughter, apparently unnoticed, for he was appareled similarly to the guards.

The last I had seen of him he stood waiting for the warriors who escorted me to close the gate behind them, that he might be alone with Thuvia. Could it be possible that they had escaped? I doubted it, and yet with all my heart I hoped that it might be true.

The third day of my incarceration brought a dozen warriors to escort me to the audience chamber, where Salensus Oll himself was to try me. A great number of nobles crowded the room, and among them I saw Thurid, but Matai Shang was not there.

Dejah Thoris, as radiantly beautiful as ever, sat upon a small throne beside Salensus Oll. The expression of sad hopelessness upon her dear face cut deep into my heart.

Her position beside the Jeddak of Jeddaks boded ill for her and me, and on the instant that I saw her there, there sprang to my mind the firm intention never to leave that chamber alive if I must leave her in the clutches of this powerful tyrant.

I had killed better men than Salensus Oll, and killed them with my bare hands, and now I swore to myself that I should kill him if I found that the only way to save the Princess of Helium. That it would mean almost instant death for me I cared not, except that it would remove me from further efforts in behalf of Dejah Thoris, and for this reason alone I would have chosen another way, for even

107

though I should kill Salensus Oll that act would not restore my beloved wife to her own people. I determined to wait the final outcome of the trial, that I might learn all that I could of the Okarian ruler's intentions, and then act accordingly.

Scarcely had I come before him than Salensus Oll summoned Thurid also.

"Dator Thurid," he said, "you have made a strange request of me; but, in accordance with your wishes and your promise that it will result only to my interests, I have decided to accede.

"You tell me that a certain announcement will be the means of convicting this prisoner and, at the same time, open the way to the gratification of my dearest wish."

Thurid nodded.

"Then shall I make the announcement here before all my nobles," continued Salensus Oll. "For a year no queen has sat upon the throne beside me, and now it suits me to take to wife one who is reputed the most beautiful woman upon Barsoom. A statement which none may truthfully deny.

"Nobles of Okar, unsheath your swords and do homage to Dejah Thoris, Princess of Helium and future Queen of Okar, for at the end of the alloted ten days she shall become the wife of Salensus Oll."

As the nobles drew their blades and lifted them on high, in accordance with the ancient custom of Okar when a jeddak announces his intention to wed, Dejah Thoris sprang to her feet and, raising her hand aloft, cried in a loud voice that they desist.

"I may not be the wife of Salensus Oll," she pleaded, "for already I be a wife and mother. John Carter, Prince of Helium, still lives. I know it to be true, for I overheard Matai Shang tell his daughter Phaidor that he had seen him in Kaor, at the court of Kulan Tith, Jeddak. A jeddak does not wed a married woman, nor will Salensus Oll thus violate the bonds of matrimony."

Salensus Oll turned upon Thurid with an ugly look.

"Is this the surprise you held in store for me?" he cried. "You assured me that no obstacle which might not be easily overcome stood between me and this woman, and now I find that the one insuperable obstacle intervenes. What mean you, man? What have you to say?"

"And should I deliver John Carter into your hands, Salensus Oll, would you not feel that I had more than satisfied the promise that I made you?" answered Thurid.

"Talk not like a fool," cried the enraged jeddak. "I am no child to be thus played with."

"I am talking only as a man who knows," replied Thurid. "Knows that he can do all that he claims."

"Then turn John Carter over to me within ten days or yourself suffer the end that I should mete out to him were he in my power!" snapped the Jeddak of Jeddaks, with an ugly scowl.

"You need not wait ten days, Salensus Oll," replied Thurid; and then, turning suddenly upon me as he extended a pointing finger, he cried: "There stands John Carter, Prince of Helium!"

"Fool!" shrieked Salensus Oll. "Fool! John Carter is a white man. This fellow be as yellow as myself. John Carter's face is smooth—Matai Shang has described him to me. This prisoner has a beard and mustache as large and black as any in Okar. Quick, guardsmen, to the pits with the black maniac who wishes to throw his life away for a poor joke upon your ruler!"

"Hold!" cried Thurid, and springing forward before I could guess his intention, he had grasped my beard and ripped the whole false fabric from my face and head, revealing my smooth, tanned skin beneath and my close-cropped black hair.

Instantly pandemonium reigned in the audience chamber of Salensus Oll. Warriors pressed forward with drawn blades, thinking that I might be contemplating the assassination of the Jeddak of Jeddaks; while others, out of curiosity to see one whose name was familiar from pole to pole, crowded behind their fellows.

As my identity was revealed I saw Dejah Thoris spring to her feet—amazement writ large upon her face—and then through that jam of armed men she forced her way before any could prevent. A moment only and she was before me with outstretched arms and eyes filled with the light of her great love.

"John Carter! John Carter!" she cried as I folded her to my breast, and then of a sudden I knew why she had denied me in the garden beneath the tower.

What a fool I had been! Expecting that she would penetrate the marvelous disguise that had been wrought for me by the barber of Marentina! She had not known me, that was all; and when she saw the sign of love from a stranger she was offended and righteously indignant. Indeed, but I had been a fool.

"And it was you," she cried, "who spoke to me from the tower! How could I dream that my beloved Virginian lay behind that fierce beard and that yellow skin?"

She had been wont to call me her Virginian as a term of endearment, for she knew that I loved the sound of that beautiful name, made a thousand times more beautiful and hallowed by her dear lips, and as I heard it again after all those long years my eyes became dimmed with tears and my voice choked with emotion.

But an instant did I crush that dear form to me ere Salensus Oll, trembling with rage and jealousy, shouldered his way to us.

"Seize the man," he cried to his warriors, and a hundred ruthless hands tore us apart.

Well it was for the nobles of the court of Okar that John Carter had been disarmed. As it was, a dozen of them felt the weight of my clenched fists, and I had fought my way half up the steps before the throne to which Salensus Oll had carried Dejah Thoris ere ever they could stop me.

Then I went down, fighting, beneath a half-hundred warriors; but before they had battered me into unconsciousness I heard that from the lips of Dejah Thoris that made all my suffering well worth while.

Standing there beside the great tyrant, who clutched her by the arm, she pointed to where I fought alone against such awful odds.

"Think you, Salensus Oll, that the wife of such as he is," she cried, "would ever dishonor his memory, were he a thousand times dead, by mating with a lesser mortal? Lives there upon any world such another as John Carter, Prince of Helium? Lives there another man who could fight his way back and forth across a warlike planet, facing savage beasts and hordes of savage men, for the love of a woman?

"I, Dejah Thoris, Princess of Helium, am his. He fought for me and won me. If you be a brave man you will honor the bravery that is his, and you will not kill him. Make him a slave if you will, Salensus Oll; but spare his life. I would rather be a slave with such as he than be Queen of Okar."

"Neither slave nor queen dictates to Salensus Oll," replied the Jeddak of Jeddaks. "John Carter shall die a natural death in the Pit of Plenty, and the day he dies Dejah Thoris shall become my queen."

I did not hear her reply, for it was then that a blow upon my head brought unconsciousness, and when I recovered my senses only a handful of guardsmen remained in the audience chamber with me. As I opened my eyes they goaded me with the points of their swords and bade me rise.

Then they led me through long corridors to a court far toward the center of the palace.

In the center of the court was a deep pit, near the edge of which stood half a dozen other guardsmen, awaiting me. One of them carried a long rope in his hands, which he commenced to make ready as we approached.

We had come to within fifty feet of these men when I felt a sudden strange and rapid pricking sensation in one of my fingers.

For a moment I was nonplused by the odd feeling, and then there came to me recollection of that which in the stress of my adventure I had entirely forgotten—the gift ring of Prince Talu of Marentina.

Instantly I looked toward the group we were nearing, at at the same time raising my left hand to my forehead, that the ring might be visible to one who sought it. Simultaneously one of the waiting warriors raised his left hand, ostensibly to brush back his hair, and upon one of his fingers I saw the duplicate of my own ring.

A quick look of intelligence passed between us, after which I kept my eyes turned away from the warrior and did not look at him again, for fear that I might arouse the suspicion of the Okarians.

When we reached the edge of the pit I saw that it was very deep, and presently I realized I was soon to judge just how far it extended below the surface of the court, for he who held the rope passed it about my body in such a way that it could be released from above at any time; and then, as all the warriors grasped it, he pushed me forward, and I fell into the yawning abyss.

After the first jerk as I reached the end of the rope that

111

had been paid out to let me fall below the pit's edge they lowered me quickly but smoothly. The moment before the plunge, while two or three of the men had been assisting in adjusting the rope about me, one of them had brought his mouth close to my cheek, and in the brief interval before I was cast into the forbidding hole he breathed a single word into my ear:

"Courage!"

The pit, which my imagination had pictured as bottomless, proved to be not more than a hundred feet in depth; but as its walls were smoothly polished it might as well have been a thousand feet, for I could never hope to escape without outside assistance.

For a day I was left in darkness; and then, quite suddenly, a brilliant light illumined my strange cell. I was reasonably hungry and thirsty by this time, not having tasted food or drink since the day prior to my incarceration.

To my amazement I found the sides of the pit, that I had thought smooth, lined with shelves, upon which were the most delicious viands and liquid refreshments that Okar afforded.

With an exclamation of delight I sprang forward to partake of some of the welcome food, but ere ever I reached it the light was extinguished, and, though I groped my way about the chamber, my hands came in contact with nothing beside the smooth, hard wall that I had felt on my first examination of my prison.

Immediately the pangs of hunger and thirst began to assail me. Where before I had had but a mild craving for food and drink, I now actually suffered for want of it, and all because of the tantalizing sight that I had had of food almost within my grasp.

Once more darkness and silence enveloped me, a silence that was broken only by a single mocking laugh.

For another day nothing occurred to break the monotony of my imprisonment or relieve the suffering superinduced by hunger and thirst. Slowly the pangs became less keen, as suffering deaded the activity of certain nerves; and then the light flashed on once again, and before me stood an array of new and tempting dishes, with great bottles of clear water and flagons of refreshing wine, upon the outside of which the cold sweat of condensation stood.

Again, with the hunger madness of a wild beast, I sprang forward to seize those tempting dishes; but, as before, the light went out and I came to a sudden stop against a hard wall.

Then the mocking laugh rang out for a second time.

The Pit of Plenty!

Ah, what a cruel mind must have devised this exquisite, hellish torture! Day after day was the thing repeated, until I was on the verge of madness; and then, as I had done in the pits of the Warhoons, I took a new, firm hold upon my reason and forced it back into the channels of sanity.

By sheer will-power I regained control over my tottering mentality, and so successful was I that the next time that the light came I sat quite still and looked indifferently at the fresh and tempting food almost within my reach. Glad I was that I had done so, for it gave me an opportunity to solve the seeming mystery of those vanishing banquets.

As I made no move to reach the food, the torturers left the light turned on in the hope that at last I could refrain no longer from giving them the delicious thrill of enjoyment that my former futile efforts to obtain it had caused.

And as I sat scrutinizing the laden shelves I presently saw how the thing was accomplished, and so simple was it that I wondered I had not guessed it before. The wall of my prison was of clearest glass—behind the glass were the tantalizing viands.

After nearly an hour the light went out, but this time there was no mocking laughter—at least not upon the part of my tormentors; but I, to be at quits with them, gave a low laugh that none might mistake for the cackle of a maniac.

Nine days passed, and I was weak from hunger and thirst, but no longer suffering—I was past that. Then, down through the darkness above, a little parcel fell to the floor at my side.

Indifferently I groped for it, thinking it but some new invention of my jailers to add to my sufferings.

At last I found it—a tiny package wrapped in paper, at the end of a strong and slender cord. As I opened it a few lozenges fell to the floor. As I gathered them up, feeling of them and smelling of them, I discovered that they were tablets of concentrated food such as are quite common in all parts of Barsoom.

Poison! I thought.

Well, what of it? Why not end my misery now rather than drag out a few more wretched days in this dark pit? Slowly I raised one of the little pellets to my lips.

"Good-bye, my Dejah Thoris!" I breathed. "I have lived for you and fought for you, and now my next dearest wish is to be realized, for I shall die for you," and, taking the morsel in my mouth, I devoured it.

One by one I ate them all, nor ever did anything taste better than those tiny bits of nourishment, within which I knew must lie the seeds of death—possibly of some hideous, torturing death.

As I sat quietly upon the floor of my prison, waiting for the end, my fingers by accident came in contact with the bit of paper in which the things had been wrapped; and as I idly played with it, my mind roaming far back into the past, that I might live again for a few brief moments before I died some of the many happy moments of a long and happy life, I became aware of strange protuberances upon the smooth surface of the parchment-like substance in my hands.

For a time they carried no special significance to my mind—I merely was mildly wondrous that they were there; but at last they seemed to take form, and then I realized that there was but a single line of them, like writing.

Now, more interestedly, my fingers traced and retraced them. There were four separate and distinct combinations of raised lines. Could it be that these were four words, and that they were intended to carry a message to me?

The more I thought of it the more excited I became, until my fingers raced madly back and forth over those bewildering little hills and valleys upon that bit of paper.

But I could make nothing of them, and at last I decided that my very haste was preventing me from solving the mystery. Then I took it more slowly. Again and again my forefinger traced the first of those four combinations.

Martian writing is rather difficult to explain to an Earth man—it is something of a cross between shorthand and picture-writing, and is an entirely different language from the spoken language of Mars.

Upon Barsoom there is but a single oral language.

114

It is spoken today by every race and nation, just as it was at the beginning of human life upon Barsoom. It has grown with the growth of the planet's learning and scientific achievements, but so ingenious a thing it is that new words to express new thoughts or describe new conditions or discoveries form themselves—no other word could explain the thing that a new word is required for other than the word that naturally falls to it, and so, no matter how far removed two nations or races, their spoken languages are identical.

Not so their written languages, however. No two nations have the same written language, and often cities of the same nation have a written language that differs greatly from that of the nation to which they belong.

Thus it was that the signs upon the paper, if in reality they were words, baffled me for some time; but at last I made out the first one.

It was "courage," and it was written in the letters of Marentina.

Courage!

That was the word the yellow guardsman had whispered in my ear as I stood upon the verge of the Pit of Plenty.

The message must be from him, and he I knew was a friend.

With renewed hope I bent my every energy to the deciphering of the balance of the message, and at last success rewarded my endeavor—I had read the four words:

"Courage! Follow the rope."

"FOLLOW THE ROPE!"

WHAT could it mean?

"Follow the rope." What rope?

Presently I recalled the cord that had been attached to the parcel when it fell at my side, and after a little groping my hand came in contact with it again. It depended from above, and when I pulled upon it I discovered that it was rigidly fastened, possibly at the pit's mouth.

Upon examination I found that the cord, though small, was amply able to sustain the weight of several men. Then I made another discovery—there was a second message knotted in the rope at about the height of my head. This I deciphered more easily, now that the key was mine.

"Bring the rope with you. Beyond the knots lies danger."

That was all there was to this message. It was evidently hastily formed—an afterthought.

I did not pause longer than to learn the contents of the second message, and, though I was none too sure of the meaning of the final admonition, "Beyond the knots lies danger," yet I was sure that here before me lay an avenue of escape, and that the sooner I took advantage of it the more likely was I to win to liberty.

At least, I could be but little worse off than I had been in the Pit of Plenty.

I was to find, however, ere I was well out of that damnable hole that I might have been very much worse off had I been compelled to remain there another two minutes.

It had taken me about that length of time to ascend some fifty feet above the bottom when a noise above attracted my attention. To my chagrin I saw that the covering of the pit was being removed far above me, and in the light of the courtyard beyond I saw a number of yellow warriors.

Could it be that I was laboriously working my way into some new trap? Were the messages spurious, after all? And then, just as my hope and courage had ebbed to their lowest, I saw two things.

One was the body of a huge, struggling, snarling apt being lowered over the side of the pit toward me, and the other was an aperture in the side of the shaft—an aperture larger than a man's body, into which my rope led.

Just as I scrambled into the dark hole before me the apt passed me, reaching out with his mighty hands to clutch me, and snapping, growling, and roaring in a most frightful manner.

Plainly now I saw the end for which Salensus Oll had destined me. After first torturing me with starvation he had caused this fierce beast to be lowered into my prison to finish the work that the jeddak's hellish imagination had conceived.

And then another truth flashed upon me—I had lived nine days of the allotted ten which must intervene before Salensus Oll could make Dejah Thoris his queen. The purpose of the apt was to insure my death before the tenth day.

I almost laughed aloud as I thought how Salensus Oll's measure of safety was to aid in defeating the very end he sought, for when they discovered that the apt was alone in the Pit of Plenty they could not know but that he had completely devoured me, and so no suspicion of my escape would cause a search to be made for me.

Coiling the rope that had carried me thus far upon my strange journey, I sought for the other end, but found that as I followed it forward it extended always before me. So this was the meaning of the words: "Follow the rope."

The tunnel through which I crawled was low and dark. I had followed it for several hundred yards when I felt a knot beneath my fingers. "Beyond the knots lies danger."

Now I went with the utmost caution, and a moment later a sharp turn in the tunnel brought me to an opening into a large, brilliantly lighted chamber.

The trend of the tunnel I had been traversing had been slightly upward, and from this I judged that the chamber into which I now found myself looking must be either on the first floor of the palace or directly beneath the first floor.

Upon the opposite wall were many strange instruments and devices, and in the center of the room stood a long table, at which two men were seated in earnest conversation.

He who faced me was a yellow man—a little, wizened-

117

up, pasty-faced old fellow with great eyes that showed the white round the entire circumference of the iris.

His companion was a black man, and I did not need to see his face to know that it was Thurid, for there was no other of the First Born north of the ice-barrier.

Thurid was speaking as I came within hearing of the men's voices.

"Solan," he was saying, "there is no risk and the reward is great. You know that you hate Salensus Oll and that nothing would please you more than to thwart him in some cherished plan. There be nothing that he more cherishes today than the idea of wedding the beautiful Princess of Helium; but I, too, want her, and with your help I may win her.

"You need not more than step from this room for an instant when I give you the signal. I will do the rest, and then, when I am gone, you may come and throw the great switch back into its place, and all will be as before. I need but an hour's start to be safe beyond the devilish power that you control in this hidden chamber beneath the palace of your master. See how easy," and with the words the black dator rose from his seat and, crossing the room, laid his hand upon a large, burnished lever that protruded from the opposite wall.

"No! No!" cried the little old man, springing after him, with a wild shriek. "Not that one! Not that one! That controls the sunray tanks, and should you pull it too far down, all Kadabra would be consumed by heat before I could replace it. Come away! Come away! You know not with what mighty powers you play. This is the lever that you seek. Note well the symbol inlaid in white upon its ebon surface."

Thurid approached and examined the handle of the lever.

"Ah, a magnet," he said. "I will remember. It is settled than I take it," he continued.

The old man hesitated. A look of combined greed and apprehension overspread his none too beautiful features.

"Double the figure," he said. "Even that were all too small an amount for the service you ask. Why, I risk my life by even entertaining you here within the forbidden precincts of my station. Should Salensus Oll learn of it he would have me thrown to the apts before the day was done."

"He dare not do that, and you know it full well, Solan,"

118

contradicted the black. "Too great a power of life and death you hold over the people of Kadabra for Salensus Oll ever to risk threatening you with death. Before ever his minions could lay their hands upon you, you might seize this very lever from which you have just warned me and wipe out the entire city."

"And myself into the bargain," said Solan, with a shudder.

"But if you were to die, anyway, you would find the nerve to do it," replied Thurid.

"Yes," muttered Solan, "I have often thought upon that very thing. Well, First Born, is your red princess worth the price I ask for my services, or will you go without her and see her in the arms of Salensus Oll tomorrow night?"

"Take your price, yellow man," replied Thurid, with an oath. "Half now and the balance when you have fulfilled your contract."

With that the dator threw a well-filled money-pouch upon the table.

Solan opened the pouch and with trembling fingers counted its contents. His weird eyes assumed a greedy expression, and his unkempt beard and mustache twitched with the muscles of his mouth and chin. It was quite evident from his very mannerism that Thurid had keenly guessed the man's weakness—even the clawlike, clutching movement of the fingers betokened the avariciousness of the miser.

Having satisfied himself that the amount was correct, Solan replaced the money in the pouch and rose from the table.

"Now," he said, "are you quite sure that you know the way to your destination? You must travel quickly to cover the ground to the cave and from thence beyond the Great Power, all within a brief hour, for no more dare I spare you."

"Let me repeat it to you," said Thurid, "that you may see if I be letter-perfect."

"Proceed," replied Solan.

"Through yonder door," he commenced, pointing to a door at the far end of the apartment, "I follow a corridor, passing three diverging corridors upon my right; then into the fourth right-hand corridor straight to where three corridors meet; here again I follow to the right, hugging the left wall closely to avoid the pit.

"At the end of this corridor I shall come to a spiral

119

runway, which I must follow down instead of up; after that the way is along but a single branchless corridor. Am I right?"

"Quite right, Dator," answered Solan; "and now begone. Already have you tempted fate too long within this forbidden place."

"Tonight, or tomorrow, then, you may expect the signal," said Thurid, rising to go.

"Tonight, or tomorrow," repeated Solan, and as the door closed behind his guest the old man continued to mutter as he turned back to the table, where he again dumped the contents of the money-pouch, running his fingers through the heap of shining metal; piling the coins into little towers; counting, recounting, and fondling the wealth the while he muttered on and on in a crooning undertone.

Presently his fingers ceased their play; his eyes popped wider than ever as they fastened upon the door through which Thurid had disappeared. The croon changed to a querulous muttering, and finally to an ugly growl.

Then the old man rose from the table, shaking his fist at the closed door. Now he raised his voice, and his words came distinctly.

"Fool!" he muttered. "Think you that for your happiness Solan will give up his life? If you escaped, Salensus Oll would know that only through my connivance could you have succeeded. Then would he send for me. What would you have me do? Reduce the city and myself to ashes? No, fool, there is a better way—a better way for Solan to keep thy money and be revenged upon Salensus Oll."

He laughed in a nasty, cackling note.

"Poor fool! You may throw the great switch that will give you the freedom of the air of Okar, and then, in fatuous security, go on with thy red princess to the freedom of—death. When you have passed beyond this chamber in your flight, what can prevent Solan replacing the switch as it was before your vile hand touched it? Nothing; and then the Guardian of the North will claim you and your woman, and Salensus Oll, when he sees your dead bodies, will never dream that the hand of Solan had aught to do with the thing."

Then his voice dropped once more into mutterings that I could not translate, but I had heard enough to cause me to guess a great deal more, and I thanked the kind Providence that had led me to this chamber at a time so filled with importance to Dejah Thoris and myself as this.

But how to pass the old man now! The cord, almost invisible upon the floor, stretched straight across the apartment to a door upon the far side.

There was no other way of which I knew, nor could I afford to ignore the advice to "follow the rope." I must cross this room, but however I should accomplish it undetected with that old man in the very center of it baffled me.

Of course I might have sprung in upon him and with my bare hands silenced him forever, but I had heard enough to convince me that with him alive the knowledge that I had gained might serve me at some future moment, while should I kill him and another be stationed in his place Thurid would not come hither with Dejah Thoris, as was quite evidently his intention.

As I stood in the dark shadow of the tunnel's end racking my brain for a feasible plan the while I watched, catlike, the old man's every move, he took up the money-pouch and crossed to one end of the apartment, where, bending to his knees, he fumbled with a panel in the wall.

Instantly I guessed that here was the hiding place in which he hoarded his wealth, and while he bent there, his back toward me, I entered the chamber upon tiptoe, and with the utmost stealth essayed to reach the opposite side before he should complete his task and turn again toward the room's center.

Scarcely thirty steps, all told, must I take, and yet it seemed to my overwrought imagination that that farther wall was miles away; but at last I reached it, nor once had I taken my eyes from the back of the old miser's head.

He did not turn until my hand was upon the button that controlled the door through which my way led, and then he turned away from me as I passed through and gently closed the door.

For an instant I paused, my ear close to the panel, to learn if he had suspected aught, but as no sound of pursuit came from within I wheeled and made my way along the new corridor, following the rope, which I coiled and brought with me as I advanced.

But a short distance farther on I came to the rope's end

at a point where five corridors met. What was I to do? Which way should I turn? I was nonplused.

A careful examination of the end of the rope revealed the fact that it had been cleanly cut with some sharp instrument. This fact and the words that had cautioned me that danger lay beyond the *knots* convinced me that the rope had been severed since my friend had placed it as my guide, for I had but passed a single knot, whereas there had evidently been two or more in the entire length of the cord.

Now, indeed, was I in a pretty fix, for neither did I know which avenue to follow nor when danger lay directly in my path; but there was nothing else to be done than follow one of the corridors, for I could gain nothing by remaining where I was.

So I chose the central opening, and passed on into its gloomy depths with a prayer upon my lips.

The floor of the tunnel rose rapidly as I advanced, and a moment later the way came to an abrupt end before a heavy door.

I could hear nothing beyond, and, with my accustomed rashness, pushed the portal wide to step into a room filled with yellow warriors.

The first to see me opened his eyes wide in astonishment, and at the same instant I felt the tingling sensation in my finger that denoted the presence of a friend of the ring.

Then others saw me, and there was a concerted rush to lay hands upon me, for these were all members of the palace guard—men familiar with my face.

The first to reach me was the wearer of the mate to my strange ring, and as he came close he whispered: "Surrender to me!" then in a loud voice shouted: "You are my prisoner, white man," and menaced me with his two weapons.

And so John Carter, Prince of Helium, meekly surrendered to a single antagonist. The others now swarmed about us, asking many questions, but I would not talk to them, and finally my captor announced that he would lead me back to my cell.

An officer ordered several other warriors to accompany him, and a moment later we were retracing the way I had just come. My friend walked close beside me, asking many silly questions about the country from which I had come, until finally his fellows paid no further attention to him or his gabbling.

Gradually, as he spoke, he lowered his voice, so that presently he was able to converse with me in a low tone without attracting attention. His ruse was a clever one, and showed that Talu had not misjudged the man's fitness for the dangerous duty upon which he was detailed.

When he had fully assured himself that the other guardsmen were not listening, he asked me why I had not followed the rope, and when I told him that it had ended at the five corridors he said that it must have been cut by someone in need of a piece of rope, for he was sure that "the stupid Kadabrans would never have guessed its purpose."

Before we had reached the spot from which the five corridors diverge my Marentinian friend had managed to drop to the rear of the little column with me, and when we came in sight of the branching ways he whispered:

"Run up the first upon the right. It leads to the watchtower upon the south wall. I will direct the pursuit up the next corridor," and with that he gave me a great shove into the dark mouth of the tunnel, at the same time crying out in simulated pain and alarm as he threw himself upon the floor as though I had felled him with a blow.

From behind the voices of the excited guardsmen came reverberating along the corridor, suddenly growing fainter as Talu's spy led them up the wrong passageway in fancied pursuit.

As I ran for my life through the dark galleries beneath the palace of Salensus Oll I must indeed have presented a remarkable appearance had there been any to note it, for though death loomed large about me, my face was split by a broad grin as I thought of the resourcefulness of the nameless hero of Marentina to whom I owed my life.

Of such stuff are the men of my beloved Helium, and when I meet another of their kind, of whatever race or color, my heart goes out to him as it did now to my new friend who had risked his life for me simply because I wore the mate to the ring his ruler had put upon his finger.

The corridor along which I ran led almost straight for a considerable distance, terminating at the foot of a spiral runway, up which I proceeded to emerge presently into a circular chamber upon the first floor of a tower.

In this apartment a dozen red slaves were employed polishing or repairing the weapons of the yellow men. The walls of the room were lined with racks in which were hundreds of straight and hooked swords, javelins, and daggers. It was evidently an armory. There were but three warriors guarding the workers.

My eyes took in the entire scene at a glance. Here were weapons in plenty! Here were sinewy red warriors to wield them!

And here now was John Carter, Prince of Helium, in need both of weapons and warriors!

As I stepped into the apartment, guards and prisoners saw me simultaneously.

Close to the entrance where I stood was a rack of straight swords, and as my hand closed upon the hilt of one of them my eyes fell upon the faces of two of the prisoners who worked side by side.

One of the guards started toward me. "Who are you?" he demanded. "What do you here?"

"I come for Tardos Mors, Jeddak of Helium, and his son, Mors Kajak," I cried, pointing to the two red prisoners, who had now sprung to their feet, wide-eyed in astonished recognition.

"Rise, red men! Before we die let us leave a memorial in the palace of Okar's tyrant that will stand forever in the annals of Kadabra to the honor and glory of Helium," for I had seen that all the prisoners there were men of Tardos Mors's navy.

Then the first guardsman was upon me and the fight was on, but scarce did we engage ere, to my horrow, I saw that the red slaves were shackled to the floor.

THE MAGNET SWITCH

THE guardsmen paid not the slightest attention to their wards, for the red men could not move over two feet from the great rings to which they were padlocked, though each had seized a weapon upon which he had been engaged when I entered the room, and stood ready to join me could they have but done so.

The yellow men devoted all their attention to me, nor were they long in discovering that the three of them were none too many to defend the armory against John Carter. Would that I had had my own good long-sword in my hand that day; but, as it was, I rendered a satisfactory account of myself with the unfamiliar weapon of the yellow man.

At first I had a time of it dodging their villainous hook-swords, but after a minute or two I had succeeded in wresting a second straight sword from one of the racks along the wall, and thereafter, using it to parry the hooks of my antagonists, I felt more evenly equipped.

The three of them were on me at once, and but for a lucky circumstance my end might have come quickly. The foremost guardsman made a vicious lunge for my side with his hook after the three of them had backed me against the wall, but as I sidestepped and raised my arm his weapon but grazed my side, passing into a rack of javelins, where it became entangled.

Before he could release it I had run him through, and then, falling back upon the tactics that have saved me a hundred times in tight pinches, I rushed the two remaining warriors, forcing them back with a perfect torrent of cuts and thrusts, weaving my sword in and out about their guards until I had the fear of death upon them.

Then one of them commenced calling for help, but it was too late to save them.

They were as putty in my hands now, and I backed them about the armory as I would until I had them where I wanted them—within reach of the swords of the shackled slaves. In an instant both lay dead upon the floor. But their cries had not been entirely fruitless, for now I heard answering shouts and the footfalls of many men running and the clank of accouterments and the commands of officers.

"The door! Quick, John Carter, bar the door!" cried Tardos Mors.

Already the guard was in sight, charging across the open court that was visible through the doorway.

A dozen seconds would bring them into the tower. A single leap carried me to the heavy portal. With a resounding bang I slammed it shut.

"The bar!" shouted Tardos Mors.

I tried to slip the huge fastening into place, but it defied my every attempt.

"Raise it a little to release the catch," cried one of the red men.

I could hear the yellow warriors leaping along the flagging just beyond the door. I raised the bar and shot it to the right just as the foremost of the guardsmen threw himself against the opposite side of the massive panels.

The barrier held—I had been in time, but by the fraction of a second only.

Now I turned my attention to the prisoners. To Tardos Mors I went first, asking where the keys might be which would unfasten their fetters.

"The officer of the guard has them," replied the Jeddak of Helium, "and he is among those without who seek entrance. You will have to force them."

Most of the prisoners were already hacking at their bonds with the swords in their hands. The yellow men were battering at the door with javelins and axes.

I turned my attention to the chains that held Tardos Mors. Again and again I cut deep into the metal with my sharp blade, but ever faster and faster fell the torrent of blows upon the portal.

At last a link parted beneath my efforts, and a moment later Tardos Mors was free, though a few inches of trailing chain still dangled from his ankle.

A splinter of wood falling inward from the door announced the headway that our enemies were making toward us.

126

The mighty panels trembled and bent beneath the furious onslaught of the enraged yellow men.

What with the battering upon the door and the hacking of the red men at their chains the din within the armory was appalling. No sooner was Tardos Mors free than he turned his attention to another of the prisoners, while I set to work to liberate Mors Kajak.

We must work fast if we would have all those fetters cut before the door gave way. Now a panel crashed inward upon the floor, and Mors Kajak sprang to the opening to defend the way until we should have time to release the others.

With javelins snatched from the wall he wrought havoc among the foremost of the Okarians while we battled with the insensate metal that stood between our fellows and freedom.

At length all but one of the prisoners were freed, and then the door fell with a mighty crash before a hastily improvised battering-ram, and the yellow horde was upon us.

"To the upper chambers!" shouted the red man who was still fettered to the floor. "To the upper chambers! There you may defend the tower against all Kadabra. Do not delay because of me, who could pray for no better death than in the service of Tardos Mors and the Prince of Helium."

But I would have sacrificed the life of every man of us rather than desert a single red man, much less the lion-hearted hero who begged us to leave him.

"Cut his chains," I cried to two of the red men, "while the balance of us hold off the foe."

There were ten of us now to do battle with the Okarian guard, and I warrant that that ancient watchtower never looked down upon a more hotly contested battle than took place that day within its own grim walls.

The first inrushing wave of yellow warriors recoiled from the slashing blades of ten of Helium's veteran fighting men. A dozen Okarian corpses blocked the doorway, but over the gruesome barrier a score more of their fellows dashed, shouting their hoarse and hideous war-cry.

Upon the bloody mound we met them, hand to hand, stabbing where the quarters were too close to cut, thrusting when we could push a foeman to arm's length; and mingled with the wild cry of the Okarian there rose and fell the glorious words: "For Helium! For Helium!" that for countless ages have spurred on the bravest of the brave to

127

those deeds of valor that have sent the fame of Helium's heroes broadcast throughout the length and breadth of a world.

Now were the fetters struck from the last of the red men, and thirteen strong we met each new charge of the soldiers of Salensus Oll. Scarce one of us but bled from a score of wounds, yet none had fallen.

From without we saw hundreds of guardsmen pouring into the courtyard, and along the lower corridor from which I had found my way to the armory we could hear the clank of metal and the shouting of men.

In a moment we should be attacked from two sides, and with all our prowess we could not hope to withstand the unequal odds which would thus divide our attention and our small numbers.

"To the upper chambers!" cried Tardos Mors, and a moment later we fell back toward the runway that led to the floors above.

Here another bloody battle was waged with the force of yellow men who charged into the armory as we fell back from the doorway. Here we lost our first man, a noble fellow whom we could ill spare; but at length all had backed into the runway except myself, who remained to hold back the Okarians until the others were safe above.

In the mouth of the narrow spiral but a single warrior could attack me at a time, so that I had little difficulty in holding them all back for the brief moment that was necessary. Then, backing slowly before them, I commenced the ascent of the spiral.

All the long way to the tower's top the guardsmen pressed me closely. When one went down before my sword another scrambled over the dead man to take his place; and thus, taking an awful toll with each few feet gained, I came to the spacious glass-walled watchtower of Kadabra.

Here my companions clustered ready to take my place, and for a moment's respite I stepped to one side while they held the enemy off.

From the lofty perch a view could be had for miles in every direction. Toward the south stretched the rugged, ice-clad waste to the edge of the mighty barrier. Toward the east and west, and dimly toward the north I descried other Okarian cities, while in the immediate foreground, just beyond the walls of Kadabra, the grim guardian shaft reared its somber head.

Then I cast my eyes down into the streets of Kadabra, from which a sudden tumult had arisen, and there I saw a battle raging, and beyond the city's walls I saw armed men marching in great columns toward a near-by gate.

Eagerly I pressed forward against the glass wall of the observatory, scarce daring to credit the testimony of my own eyes. But at last I could doubt no longer, and with a shout of joy that rose strangely in the midst of the cursing and groaning of the battling men at the entrance to the chamber, I called to Tardos Mors.

As he joined me I pointed down into the streets of Kadabra and to the advancing columns beyond, above which floated bravely in the arctic air the flags and banners of Helium.

An instant later every red man in the lofty chamber had seen the inspiring sight, and such a shout of thanksgiving arose as I warrant never before echoed through that age-old pile of stone.

But still we must fight on, for though our troops had entered Kadabra, the city was yet far from capitulation, nor had the palace been even assaulted. Turn and turn about we held the top of the runway while the others feasted their eyes upon the sight of our valiant countrymen battling far beneath us.

Now they have rushed the palace gate! Great battering-rams are dashed against its formidable surface. Now they are repulsed by a deadly shower of javelins from the wall's top!

Once again they charge, but a sortie by a large force of Okarians from an intersecting avenue crumples the head of the column, and the men of Helium go down, fighting, beneath an overwhelming force.

The palace gate flies open and a force of the jeddak's own guard, picked men from the flower of the Okarian army, sallies forth to shatter the broken regiments. For a moment it looks as though nothing could avert defeat, and then I see a noble figure upon a mighty thoat—not the tiny thoat of the red man, but one of his huge cousins of the dead sea bottoms.

The warrior hews his way to the front, and behind him rally the disorganized soldiers of Helium. As he raises his head aloft to fling a challenge at the men upon the palace walls I see his face, and my heart swells in pride and happiness as the red warriors leap to the side of their leader and win back the ground that they had but just lost—the face of him upon the mighty thoat is the face of my son—Carthoris of Helium.

At his side fights a huge Martian war-hound, nor did I need a second look to know that it was Woola—my faithful Woola who had thus well performed his arduous task and brought the succoring legions in the nick of time.

"In the nick of time?"

Who yet might say that they were not too late to save, but surely they could avenge! And such retribution as that unconquered army would deal out to the hateful Okarians! I sighed to think that I might not be alive to witness it.

Again I turned to the windows. The red men had not yet forced the outer palace wall, but they were fighting nobly against the best that Okar afforded—valiant warriors who contested every inch of the way.

Now my attention was caught by a new element without the city wall—a great body of mounted warriors looming large above the red men. They were the huge green allies of Helium—the savage hordes from the dead sea bottoms of the far south.

In grim and terrible silence they sped on toward the gate, the padded hoofs of their frightful mounts giving forth no sound. Into the doomed city they charged, and as they wheeled across the wide plaza before the palace of the Jeddak of Jeddaks I saw, riding at their head, the mighty figure of their mighty leader—Tars Tarkas, Jeddak of Thark.

My wish, then, was to be gratified, for I was to see my old friend battling once again, and though not shoulder to shoulder with him, I, too, would be fighting in the same cause here in the high tower of Okar.

Nor did it seem that our foes would ever cease their stubborn attacks, for still they came, though the way to our chamber was often clogged with the bodies of their dead. At times they would pause long enough to drag back the impeding corpses, and then fresh warriors would forge upward to taste the cup of death.

I had been taking my turn with the others in defending the approach to our lofty retreat when Mors Kajak, who had been watching the battle in the street below, called aloud in sudden excitement. There was a note of apprehension in his voice that brought me to his side the instant that I could turn my place over to another, and as I reached him he pointed far out across the waste of snow and ice toward the southern horizon.

"Alas!" he cried, "that I should be forced to witness cruel fate betray them without power to warn or aid; but they be past either now."

As I looked in the direction he indicated I saw the cause of his perturbation. A mighty fleet of fliers was approaching majestically toward Kadabra from the direction of the ice-barrier. On and on they came with ever increasing velocity.

"The grim shaft that they call the Guardian of the North is beckoning to them," said Mors Kajak sadly, "just as it beckoned to Tardos Mors and his great fleet; see where they lie, crumpled and broken, a grim and terrible monument to the mighty force of destruction which naught can resist."

I, too, saw; but something else I saw that Mors Kajak did not; in my mind's eye I saw a buried chamber whose walls were lined with strange instruments and devices.

In the center of the chamber was a long table, and before it sat a little, pop-eyed old man counting his money; but, plainest of all, I saw upon the wall a great switch with a small magnet inlaid within the surface of its black handle.

Then I glanced out at the fast-approaching fleet. In five minutes that mighty armada of the skies would be bent and worthless scrap, lying at the base of the shaft beyond the city's wall, and yellow hordes would be loosed from another gate to rush out upon the few survivors stumbling blindly down through the mass of wreckage; then the apts would come. I shuddered at the thought, for I could vividly picture the whole horrible scene.

Quick have I always been to decide and act. The impulse that moves me and the doing of the thing seem simultaneous; for if my mind goes through the tedious formality of reasoning, it must be a subconscious act of which I am not objectively aware. Psychologists tell me that, as the subconscious does not reason, too close a scrutiny of my mental activities might prove anything but flattering; but be that as it may, I have often won success while the thinker would have been still at the endless task of comparing various judgments.

And now celerity of action was the prime essential to the success of the thing that I had decided upon.

Grasping my sword more firmly in my hand, I called to the red man at the opening to the runway to stand aside.

"Way for the Prince of Helium!" I shouted; and before the astonished yellow man whose misfortune it was to be at the fighting end of the line at that particular moment could gather his wits together my sword had decapitated him, and I was rushing like a mad bull down upon those behind him.

"Way for the Prince of Helium!" I shouted as I cut a path through the astonished guardsmen of Salensus Oll.

Hewing to right and left, I beat my way down that warrior-choked spiral until, near the bottom, those below, thinking that an army was descending upon them, turned and fled.

The armory at the first floor was vacant when I entered it, the last of the Okarians having fled into the courtyard, so none saw me continue down the spiral toward the corridor beneath.

Here I ran as rapidly as my legs would carry me toward the five corners, and there plunged into the passageway that led to the station of the old miser.

Without the formality of a knock, I burst into the room. There sat the old man at his table; but as he saw me he sprang to his feet, drawing his sword.

With scarce more than a glance toward him I leaped for the great switch; but, quick as I was, that wiry old fellow was there before me.

How he did it I shall never know, nor does it seem credible that any Martian-born creature could approximate the marvelous speed of my earthly muscles.

Like a tiger he turned upon me, and I was quick to see why Solan had been chosen for this important duty.

Never in all my life have I seen such wondrous swordsmanship and such uncanny agility as that ancient bag of bones displayed. He was in forty places at the same time, and before I had half a chance to awaken to my danger he was like to have made a monkey of me, and a dead monkey at that.

It is strange how new and unexpected conditions bring out unguessed ability to meet them.

That day in the buried chamber beneath the palace of Salensus Oll I learned what swordsmanship meant, and to what heights of sword mastery I could achieve when pitted against such a wizard of the blade as Solan.

For a time he liked to have bested me; but presently the latent possibilities that must have been lying dormant within me for a lifetime came to the fore, and I fought as I had never dreamed a human being could fight.

That that duel-royal should have taken place in the dark recesses of a cellar, without a single appreciative eye to witness it has always seemed to me almost a world calamity—at least from the viewpoint Barsoomian, where bloody strife is the first and greatest consideration of individuals, nations, and races.

I was fighting to reach the switch, Solan to prevent me; and, though we stood not three feet from it, I could not win an inch toward it, nor he force me back an inch for the first five minutes of our battle.

I knew that if I were to throw it in time to save the oncoming fleet it must be done in the next few seconds, and so I tried my old rushing tactics; but I might as well have rushed a brick wall for all that Solan gave way.

In fact, I came near to impaling myself upon his point for my pains; but right was on my side, and I think that that must give a man greater confidence than though he knew himself to be battling in a wicked cause.

At least, I did not want in confidence; and when I next rushed Solan it was to one side with implicit confidence that he must turn to meet my new line of attack, and turn he did, so that now we fought with our sides towards the coveted goal—the great switch stood within my reach upon my right hand.

To uncover my breast for an instant would have been to court sudden death, but I saw no other way than to chance it, if by so doing I might rescue that oncoming, succoring fleet; and so, in the face of a wicked sword-thrust, I reached out my point and caught the great switch a sudden blow that released it from its seating.

So surprised and horrified was Solan that he forgot to finish his thrust; instead, he wheeled toward the switch with a loud shriek—a shriek which was his last, for before his hand could touch the lever it sought, my sword's point had passed through his heart.

133

THE TIDE OF BATTLE

BUT Solan's last loud cry had not been without effect, for a moment later a dozen guardsmen burst into the chamber, though not before I had so bent and demolished the great switch that it could not be again used to turn the powerful current into the mighty magnet of destruction it controlled.

The result of the sudden coming of the guardsmen had been to compel me to seek seclusion in the first passageway that I could find, and that to my disappointment proved to be not the one with which I was familiar, but another upon its left.

They must have either heard or guessed which way I went, for I had proceeded but a short distance when I heard the sound of pursuit. I had no mind to stop and fight these men here when there was fighting aplenty elsewhere in the city of Kadabra—fighting that could be of much more avail to me and mine than useless life-taking far below the palace.

But the fellows were pressing me; and as I did not know the way at all, I soon saw that they would overtake me unless I found a place to conceal myself until they had passed, which would then give me an opportunity to return the way I had come and regain the tower, or possibly find a way to reach the city streets.

The passageway had risen rapidly since leaving the apartment of the switch, and now ran level and well lighted straight into the distance as far as I could see. The moment that my pursuers reached this straight stretch I would be in plain sight of them, with no chance to escape from the corridor undetected.

Presently I saw a series of doors opening from either side of the corridor, and as they all looked alike to me I tried the first one that I reached. It opened into a small chamber, luxuriously furnished, and was evidently an ante-chamber off some office or audience chamber of the palace.

On the far side was a heavily curtained doorway beyond which I heard the hum of voices. Instantly I crossed the small chamber, and, parting the curtains, looked within the larger apartment.

Before me were a party of perhaps fifty gorgeously clad nobles of the court, standing before a throne upon which sat Salensus Oll. The Jeddak of Jeddaks was addressing them.

"The allotted hour has come," he was saying as I entered the apartment; "and though the enemies of Okar be within her gates, naught may stay the will of Salensus Oll. The great ceremony must be omitted that no single man may be kept from his place in the defenses other than the fifty that custom demands shall witness the creation of a new queen in Okar.

"In a moment the thing shall have been done and we may return to the battle, while she who is now the Princess of Helium looks down from the queen's tower upon the annihilation of her former countrymen and witnesses the greatness which is her husband's."

Then, turning to a courtier, he issued some command in a low voice.

The addressed hastened to a small door at the far end of the chamber and, swinging it wide, cried: "Way for Dejah Thoris, future Queen of Okar!"

Immediately two guardsmen appeared dragging the unwilling bride toward the altar. Her hands were still manacled behind her, evidently to prevent suicide.

Her disheveled hair and panting bosom betokened that, chained though she was, still had she fought against the thing that they would do to her.

At sight of her Salensus Oll rose and drew his sword, and the sword of each of the fifty nobles was raised on high to form an arch, beneath which the poor, beautiful creature was dragged toward her doom.

A grim smile forced itself to my lips as I thought of the rude awakening that lay in store for the ruler of Okar, and my itching fingers fondled the hilt of my bloody sword.

As I watched the procession that moved slowly toward the throne—a procession which consisted of but a handful of priests, who followed Dejah Thoris and the two guardsmen—I caught a fleeting glimpse of a black face peering from behind the draperies that covered the wall back of the dais upon which stood Salensus Oll awaiting his bride.

Now the guardsmen were forcing the Princess of Helium up the few steps to the side of the tyrant of Okar, and I had no eyes and no thoughts for aught else. A priest opened a book and, raising his hand, commenced to drone out a sing-song ritual. Salensus Oll reached for the hand of his bride.

I had intended waiting until some circumstance should give me a reasonable hope of success; for, even though the entire ceremony should be completed, there could be no valid marriage while I lived. What I was most concerned in, of course, was the rescuing of Dejah Thoris—I wished to take her from the palace of Salensus Oll, if such a thing were possible; but whether it were accomplished before or after the mock marriage was a matter of secondary import.

When, however, I saw the vile hand of Salensus Oll reach out for the hand of my beloved princess I could restrain myself no longer, and before the nobles of Okar knew that aught had happened I had leaped through their thin line and was upon the dais beside Dejah Thoris and Salensus Oll.

With the flat of my sword I struck down his polluting hand; and grasping Dejah Thoris round the waist, I swung her behind me as, with my back against the draperies of the dais, I faced the tyrant of the north and his roomful of noble warriors.

The Jeddak of Jeddaks was a great mountain of a man—a coarse, brutal beast of a man—and as he towered above me there, his fierce black whiskers and mustache bristling in rage, I can well imagine that a less seasoned warrior might have trembled before him.

With a snarl he sprang toward me with naked sword, but whether Salensus Oll was a good swordsman or a poor I never learned; for with Dejah Thoris at my back I was no longer human—I was a superman, and no man could have withstood me then.

With a single, low: "For the Princess of Helium!" I ran my blade straight through the rotten heart of Okar's rotten ruler, and before the white, drawn faces of his nobles Salensus Oll rolled, grinning in horrible death, to the foot of the steps below his marriage throne.

For a moment tense silence reigned in the nuptial-room. Then the fifty nobles rushed upon me. Furiously we fought, but the advantage was mine, for I stood upon a raised platform above them, and I fought for the most glorious woman of a glorious race, and I fought for a great love and for the mother of my boy.

And from behind my shoulder, in the silvery cadence of that dear voice, rose the brave battle anthem of Helium which the nation's women sing as their men march out to victory.

That alone was enough to inspire me to victory over even greater odds, and I verily believe that I should have bested the entire roomful of yellow warriors that day in the nuptial chamber of the palace at Kadabra had not interruption come to my aid.

Fast and furious was the fighting as the nobles of Salensus Oll sprang, time and again, up the steps before the throne only to fall back before a sword hand that seemed to have gained a new wizardy from its experience with the cunning Solan.

Two were pressing me so closely that I could not turn when I heard a movement behind me, and noted that the sound of the battle anthem had ceased. Was Dejah Thoris preparing to take her place beside me?

Heroic daughter of a heroic world! It would not be unlike her to have seized a sword and fought at my side, for, though the women of Mars are not trained in the arts of war, the spirit is theirs, and they have been known to do that very thing upon countless occasions.

But she did not come, and glad I was, for it would have doubled my burden in protecting her before I should have been able to force her back again out of harm's way. She must be contemplating some cunning strategy, I thought, and so I fought on secure in the belief that my divine princess stood close behind me.

For half an hour at least I must have fought there against the nobles of Okar ere ever a one placed a foot upon the dais where I stood, and then of a sudden all that remained of them formed below me for a last, mad, desperate charge; but even as they advanced the door at the far end of the chamber swung wide and a wild-eyed messenger sprang into the room.

"The Jeddak of Jeddaks!" he cried. "Where is the Jeddak of Jeddaks? The city has fallen before the hordes from beyond the barrier, and but now the great gate of the palace itself has been forced and the warriors of the south are pouring into its sacred precincts.

"Where is Salensus Oll? He alone may revive the flagging

137

courage of our warriors. He alone may save the day for Okar. Where is Salensus Oll?"

The nobles stepped back from about the dead body of their ruler, and one of them pointed to the grinning corpse.

The messenger staggered back in horror as though from a blow in the face.

"Then fly, nobles of Okar!" he cried, "for naught can save you. Hark! They come!"

As he spoke we heard the deep roar of angry men from the corridor without, and the clank of metal and the clang of swords.

Without another glance toward me, who had stood a spectator of the tragic scene, the nobles wheeled and fled from the apartment through another exit.

Almost immediately a force of yellow warriors appeared in the doorway through which the messenger had come. They were backing toward the apartment, stubbornly resisting the advance of a handful of red men who faced them and forced them slowly but inevitably back.

Above the heads of the contestants I could see from my elevated station upon the dais the face of my old friend Kantos Kan. He was leading the little party that had won its way into the very heart of the palace of Salensus Oll.

In an instant I saw that by attacking the Okarians from the rear I could so quickly disorganize them that their further resistance would be short-lived, and with this idea in mind I sprang from the dais, casting a word of explanation to Dejah Thoris over my shoulder, though I did not turn to look at her.

With myself ever between her enemies and herself, and with Kantos Kan and his warriors winning to the apartment, there could be no danger to Dejah Thoris standing there alone beside the throne.

I wanted the men of Helium to see me and to know that their beloved princess was here, too, for I knew that this knowledge would inspire them to even greater deeds of valor than they had performed in the past, though great indeed must have been those which won for them a way into the almost impregnable palace of the tyrant of the north.

As I crossed the chamber to attack the Kadabrans from the rear a small doorway at my left opened, and, to my

138

surprise, revealed the figures of Matai Shang, Father of Thern and Phaidor, his daughter, peering into the room.

A quick glance about they took. Their eyes rested for a moment, wide in horror, upon the dead body of Salensus Oll, upon the blood that crimsoned the floor, upon the corpses of the nobles who had fallen thick before the throne, upon me, and upon the battling warriors at the other door.

They did not essay to enter the apartment, but scanned its every corner from where they stood, and then, when their eyes had sought its entire area, a look of fierce rage overspread the features of Matai Shang, and a cold and cunning smile touched the lips of Phaidor.

Then they were gone, but not before a taunting laugh was thrown directly in my face by the woman.

I did not understand then the meaning of Matai Shang's rage or Phaidor's pleasure, but I knew that neither boded good for me.

A moment later I was upon the backs of the yellow men, and as the red men of Helium saw me above the shoulders of their antagonists a great shout rang through the corridor, and for a moment drowned the noise of battle.

"For the Prince of Helium!" they cried. "For the Prince of Helium!" and, like hungry lions upon their prey, they fell once more upon the weakening warriors of the north.

The yellow men, cornered between two enemies, fought with the desperation that utter hopelessness often induces. Fought as I should have fought had I been in their stead, with the determination to take as many of my enemies with me when I died as lay within the power of my sword arm.

It was a glorious battle, but the end seemed inevitable, when presently from down the corridor behind the red men came a great body of reenforcing yellow warriors.

Now were the tables turned, and it was the men of Helium who seemed doomed to be ground between two millstones. All were compelled to turn to meet this new assault by a greatly superior force, so that to me was left the remnants of the yellow men within the throneroom.

They kept me busy, too; so busy that I began to wonder if indeed I should ever be done with them. Slowly they pressed me back into the room, and when they had all passed in after me, one of them closed and bolted the door, effectually barring the way against the men of Kantos Kan.

It was a clever move, for it put me at the mercy of a dozen men within a chamber from which assistance was locked out, and it gave the red men in the corridor beyond no avenue of escape should their new antagonists press them too closely.

But I have faced heavier odds myself than were pitted against me that day, and I knew that Kantos Kan had battled his way from a hundred more dangerous traps than that in which he now was. So it was with no feelings of despair that I turned my attention to the business of the moment.

Constantly my thoughts reverted to Dejah Thoris, and I longed for the moment when, the fighting done, I could fold her in my arms, and hear once more the words of love which had been denied me for so many years.

During the fighting in the chamber I had not even a single chance to so much as steal a glance at her where she stood behind me beside the throne of the dead ruler. I wondered why she no longer urged me on with the strains of the martial hymn of Helium; but I did not need more than the knowledge that I was battling for her to bring out the best that is in me.

It would be wearisome to narrate the details of that bloody struggle; of how we fought from the doorway, the full length of the room to the very foot of the throne before the last of my antagonists fell with my blade piercing his heart.

And then, with a glad cry, I turned with outstretched arms to seize my princess, and as my lips smothered hers to reap the reward that would be thrice ample payment for the bloody encounters through which I had passed for her dear sake from the south pole to the north.

The glad cry died, frozen upon my lips; my arms dropped limp and lifeless to my sides; as one who reels beneath the burden of a mortal wound I staggered up the steps before the throne.

Dejah Thoris was gone.

WITH the realization that Dejah Thoris was no longer within the throneroom came the belated recollection of the dark face that I had glimpsed peering from behind the draperies that backed the throne of Salensus Oll at the moment that I had first come so unexpectedly upon the strange scene being enacted within the chamber.

Why had the sight of that evil countenance not warned me to greater caution? Why had I permitted the rapid development of new situations to efface the recollection of that menacing danger? But, alas, vain regret would not erase the calamity that had befallen.

Once again had Dejah Thoris fallen into the clutches of that archfiend, Thurid, the black dator of the First Born. Again was all my arduous labor gone for naught. Now I realized the cause of the rage that had been writ so large upon the features of Matai Shang and the cruel pleasure that I had seen upon the face of Phaidor.

They had known or guessed the truth, and the hekkador of the Holy Therns, who had evidently come to the chamber in the hope of thwarting Salensus Oll in his contemplated perfidy against the high priest who coveted Dejah Thoris for himself, realized that Thurid had stolen the prize from beneath his very nose.

Phaidor's pleasure had been due to her realization of what this last cruel blow would mean to me, as well as to a partial satisfaction of her jealous hatred for the Princess of Helium.

My first thought was to look beyond the draperies at the back of the throne, for there it was that I had seen Thurid. With a single jerk I tore the priceless stuff from its fastenings, and there before me was revealed a narrow doorway behind the throne.

No question entered my mind but that here lay the opening of the avenue of escape which Thurid had followed, and had there been it would have been dissipated by the sight of a tiny, jeweled ornament which lay a few steps within the corridor beyond.

As I snatched up the bauble I saw that it bore the device of the Princess of Helium, and then pressing it to my lips I dashed madly along the winding way that led gently downward toward the lower galleries of the palace.

I had followed but a short distance when I came upon the room in which Solan formerly had held sway. His dead body still lay where I had left it, nor was there any sign that another had passed through the room since I had been there; but I knew that two had done so—Thurid, the black dator, and Dejah Thoris.

For a moment I paused uncertain as to which of the several exits from the apartment would lead me upon the right path. I tried to recollect the directions which I had heard Thurid repeat to Solan, and at last, slowly, as though through a heavy fog, the memory of the words of the First Born came to me:

"Follow a corridor, passing three diverging corridors upon the right; then into the fourth right-hand corridor to where three corridors meet; here again follow to the right, hugging the left wall closely to avoid the pit. At the end of this corridor I shall come to a spiral runway which I must follow down instead of up; after that the way is along but a single branchless corridor."

And I recalled the exit at which he had pointed as he spoke.

It did not take me long to start upon that unknown way, nor did I go with caution, although I knew that there might be grave dangers before me.

Part of the way was black as sin, but for the most it was fairly well lighted. The stretch where I must hug the left wall to avoid the pits was darkest of them all, and I was nearly over the edge of the abyss before I knew that I was near the danger spot.

A narrow ledge, scarce a foot wide, was all that had been left to carry the initiated past that frightful cavity into which the unknowing must surely have toppled at the first step. But at last I had won safely beyond it, and then a feeble light made the balance of the way plain, until, at the end of the last corridor, I came suddenly out into the glare of day upon a field of snow and ice.

Clad for the warm atmosphere of the hothouse city of Kadabra, the sudden change to arctic frigidity was anything but pleasant; but the worst of it was that I knew I could not endure the bitter cold, almost naked as I was, and that I would perish before ever I could overtake Thurid and Dejah Thoris.

To be thus blocked by nature, who had had all the arts and wiles of cunning man pitted against him, seemed a cruel fate, and as I staggered back into the warmth of the tunnel's end I was as near hopelessness as I ever have been.

I had by no means given up my intention of continuing the pursuit, for if needs be I would go ahead though I perished ere ever I reached my goal, but if there were a safer way it were well worth the delay to attempt to discover it, that I might come again to the side of Dejah Thoris in fit condition to do battle for her.

Scarce had I returned to the tunnel than I stumbled over a portion of a fur garment that seemed fastened to the floor of the corridor close to the wall. In the darkness I could not see what held it, but by groping with my hands I discovered that it was wedged beneath the bottom of a closed door.

Pushing the portal aside, I found myself upon the threshold of a small chamber, the walls of which were lined with hooks from which depended suits of the complete outdoor apparel of the yellow men.

Situated as it was at the mouth of a tunnel leading from the palace, it was quite evident that this was the dressing-room used by the nobles leaving and entering the hothouse city, and that Thurid, having knowledge of it, had stopped here to outfit himself and Dejah Thoris before venturing into the bitter cold of the arctic world beyond.

In his haste he had dropped several garments upon the floor, and the telltale fur that had fallen partly within the corridor had proved the means of guiding me to the very spot he would least have wished me to have knowledge of.

It required but the matter of a few seconds to don the necessary orluk-skin clothing, with the heavy, fur-lined boots that are so essential a part of the garmenture of one who would successfully contend with the frozen trails and the icy winds of the bleak northland.

Once more I stepped beyond the tunnel's mouth to find the fresh tracks of Thurid and Dejah Thoris in the new-fallen snow. Now, at last, was my task an easy one, for though the going was rough in the extreme, I was no longer vexed by doubts as to the direction I should follow, or harassed by darkness or hidden dangers.

Through a snow-covered cañon the way led up toward the summit of low hills. Beyond these it dipped again into another cañon, only to rise a quarter-mile farther on toward a pass which skirted the flank of a rocky hill.

I could see by the signs of those who had gone before that when Dejah Thoris had walked she had been continually holding back, and that the black man had been compelled to drag her. For other stretches only his foot-prints were visible, deep and close together in the heavy snow, and I knew from these signs that then he had been forced to carry her, and I could well imagine that she had fought him fiercely every step of the way.

As I came round the jutting promontory of the hill's shoulder I saw that which quickened my pulses and set my heart to beating high, for within a tiny basin between the crest of this hill and the next stood four people before the mouth of a great cave, and beside them upon the gleaming snow rested a flier which had evidently but just been dragged from its hiding place.

The four were Dejah Thoris, Phaidor, Thurid, and Matai Shang. The two men were engaged in a heated argument —the Father of Therns threatening, while the black scoffed at him as he went about the work at which he was engaged.

As I crept toward them cautiously that I might come as near as possible before being discovered, I saw that finally the men appeared to have reached some sort of a compromise, for with Phaidor's assistance they both set about dragging the resisting Dejah Thoris to the flier's deck.

Here they made her fast, and then both again descended to the ground to complete the preparations for departure. Phaidor entered the small cabin upon the vessel's deck.

I had come to within a quarter of a mile of them when Matai Shang espied me. I saw him seize Thurid by the shoulder, wheeling him around in my direction as he pointed to where I was now plainly visible, for the moment that I knew I had been perceived I cast aside every attempt at stealth and broke into a mad race for the flier.

The two redoubled their efforts at the propeller at which

they were working, and which very evidently was being replaced after having been removed for some purpose of repair.

They had the thing completed before I had covered half the distance that lay between me and them, and then both made a rush for the boarding-ladder.

Thurid was the first to reach it, and with the agility of a monkey clambered swiftly to the boat's deck, where a touch of the button controlling the buoyancy tanks sent the craft slowly upward, though not with the speed that marks the well-conditioned flier.

I was still some hundred yards away as I saw them rising from my grasp.

Back by the city of Kadabra lay a great fleet of mighty fliers —the ships of Helium and Ptarth that I had saved from destruction earlier in the day; but before ever I could reach them Thurid could easily make good his escape.

As I ran I saw Matai Shang clambering up the swaying, swinging ladder toward the deck, while above him leaned the evil face of the First Born. A trailing rope from the vessel's stern put new hope in me, for if I could but reach it before it whipped too high above my head there was yet a chance to gain the deck by its slender aid.

That there was something radically wrong with the flier was evident from its lack of buoyancy, and the further fact that though Thurid had turned twice to the starting lever the boat still hung motionless in the air, except for a slight drifting with a low breeze from the north.

Now Matai Shang was close to the gunwale. A long, claw-like hand was reaching up to grasp the metal rail.

Thurid leaned farther down toward his co-conspirator.

Suddenly a raised dagger gleamed in the upflung hand of the black. Down it drove toward the white face of the Father of Therns. With a loud shriek of fear the Holy Hekkador grasped frantically at that menacing arm.

I was almost to the trailing rope by now. The craft was still rising slowly, the while it drifted from me. Then I stumbled on the icy way, striking my head upon a rock as I fell sprawling but an arm's length from the rope, the end of which was now just leaving the ground.

With the blow upon my head came unconsciousness.

It could not have been more than a few seconds that I lay

senseless there upon the northern ice, while all that was dearest to me drifted farther from my reach in the clutches of that black fiend, for when I opened my eyes Thurid and Matai Shang yet battled at the ladder's top, and the flier drifted but a hundred yards farther to the south—but the end of the trailing rope was now a good thirty feet above the ground.

Goaded to madness by the cruel misfortune that had tripped me when success was almost within my grasp, I tore frantically across the intervening space, and just beneath the rope's dangling end I put my earthly muscles to the supreme test.

With a mighty, catlike bound I sprang upward toward that slender strand—the only avenue which yet remained that could carry me to my vanishing love.

A foot above its lowest end my fingers closed. Tightly as I clung I felt the rope slipping, slipping through my grasp. I tried to raise my free hand to take a second hold above my first, but the change of position that resulted caused me to slip more rapidly toward the end of the rope.

Slowly I felt the tantalizing thing escaping me. In a moment all that I had gained would be lost—then my fingers reached a knot at the very end of the rope and slipped no more.

With a prayer of gratitude upon my lips I scrambled upward toward the boat's deck. I could not see Thurid and Matai Shang now, but I heard the sounds of conflict and thus knew that they still fought—the thern for his life and the black for the incrased buoyancy that relief from the weight of even a single body would give the craft.

Should Matai Shang die before I reached the deck my chances of ever reaching it would be slender indeed, for the black dator need but cut the rope above me to be freed from me forever, for the vessel had drifted across the brink of a chasm into whose yawning depths my body would drop to be crushed to a shapeless pulp should Thurid reach the rope now.

At last my hand closed upon the ship's rail and that very instant a horrid shriek rang out below me that sent my blood cold and turned my horrified eyes downward to a shrieking, hurtling, twisting thing that shot downward into the awful chasm beneath me.

It was Matai Shang, Holy Hekkador, Father of Therns, gone to his last accounting.

Then my head came above the deck and I saw Thurid, dagger in hand, leaping toward me. He was opposite the forward end of the cabin, while I was attempting to clamber aboard near the vessel's stern. But a few paces lay between us. No power on earth could raise me to that deck before the infuriated black would be upon me.

My end had come. I knew it; but had there been a doubt in my mind the nasty leer of triumph upon that wicked face would have convinced me. Beyond Thurid I could see my Dejah Thoris, wide-eyed and horrified, struggling at her bonds. That she should be forced to witness my awful death made my bitter fate seem doubly cruel.

I ceased my efforts to climb across the gunwale. Instead I took a firm grasp upon the rail with my left hand and drew my dagger.

I should at least die as I had lived—fighting.

As Thurid came opposite the cabin's doorway a new element projected itself into the grim tragedy of the air that was being enacted upon the deck of Matai Shang's disabled flier.

It was Phaidor.

With flushed face and disheveled hair, and eyes that betrayed the recent presence of mortal tears—above which this proud goddess had always held herself—she leaped to the deck directly before me.

In her hand was a long, slim dagger. I cast a last look upon my beloved princess, smiling, as men should who are about to die. Then I turned my face up toward Phaidor —waiting for the blow.

Never have I seen that beautiful face more beautiful than it was at that moment. It seemed incredible that one so lovely could yet harbor within her fair bosom a heart so cruel and relentless, and today there was a new expression in her wondrous eyes that I never before had seen there—an unfamiliar softness, and a look of suffering.

Thurid was beside her now—pushing past to reach me first, and then what happened happened so quickly that it was all over before I could realize the truth of it.

Phaidor's slim hand shot out to close upon the black's dagger wrist. Her right hand went high with its gleaming blade.

147

"That for Matai Shang!" she cried, and she buried her blade deep in the dator's breast. "That for the wrong you would have done Dejah Thoris!" and again the sharp steel sank into the bloody flesh.

"And that, and that, and that!" she shrieked, "for John Carter, Prince of Helium," and with each word her sharp point pierced the vile heart of the great villain. Then, with a vindictive shove she cast the carcass of the First Born from the deck to fall in awful silence after the body of his victim.

I had been so paralyzed by surprise that I had made no move to reach the deck during the awe-inspiring scene which I had just witnessed, and now I was to be still further amazed by her next act, for Phaidor extended her hand to me and assisted me to the deck, where I stood gazing at her in unconcealed and stupefied wonderment.

A wan smile touched her lips—it was not the cruel and haughty smile of the goddess with which I was familiar. "You wonder, John Carter," she said, "what strange thing has wrought this change in me? I will tell you. It is love —love of you," and when I darkened my brows in disapproval of her words she raised an appealing hand.

"Wait," she said. "It is a different love from mine—it is the love of your princess, Dejah Thoris, for you that has taught me what true love may be—what it should be, and how far from real love was my selfish and jealous passion for you.

"Now am I different. Now could I love as Dejah Thoris loves, and so my only happiness can be to know that you and she are once more united, for in her alone can you find true happiness.

"But I am unhappy because of the wickedness that I have wrought. I have many sins to expiate, and though I be deathless, life is all too short for the atonement.

"But there is another way, and if Phaidor, daughter of the Holy Hekkador of the Holy Therns, has sinned she has this day already made partial reparation, and lest you doubt the sincerity of her protestations and her avowal of a new love that embraces Dejah Thoris also, she will prove her sincerity in the only way that lies open—having saved you for another, Phaidor leaves you to her embraces."

With her last word she turned and leaped from the vessel's deck into the abyss below.

With a cry of horror I sprang forward in a vain attempt to save the life that for two years I would so gladly have seen extinguished. I was too late.

With tear-dimmed eyes I turned away that I might not see the awful sight beneath.

A moment later I had struck the bonds from Dejah Thoris, and as her dear arms went about my neck and her perfect lips pressed to mine I forgot the horrors that I had witnessed and the suffering that I had endured in the rapture of my reward.

THE NEW RULER

THE flier upon whose deck Dejah Thoris and I found ourselves after twelve long years of separation proved entirely useless. Her buoyancy tanks leaked badly. Her engine would not start. We were helpless there in mid air above the arctic ice.

The craft had drifted across the chasm which held the corpses of Matai Shang, Thurid, and Phaidor, and now hung above a low hill. Opening the buoyancy escape valves I permitted her to come slowly to the ground, and as she touched, Dejah Thoris and I stepped from her deck and, hand in hand, turned back across the frozen waste toward the city of Kadabra.

Through the tunnel that had led me in pursuit of them we passed, walking slowly, for we had much to say to each other.

She told me of that last terrible moment months before when the door of her prison cell within the Temple of the Sun was slowly closing between us. Of how Phaidor had sprung upon her with uplifted dagger, and of Thuvia's shriek as she had realized the foul intention of the thern goddess.

It had been that cry that had rung in my ears all the long, weary months that I had been left in cruel doubt as to my princess' fate; for I had not known that Thuvia had wrested the blade from the daughter of Matai Shang before it had touched either Dejah Thoris or herself.

She told me, too, of the awful eternity of her imprisonment. Of the cruel hatred of Phaidor, and the tender love of Thuvia, and of how even when despair was the darkest those two red girls had clung to the same hope and belief—that John Carter would find a way to release them.

Presently we came to the chamber of Solan. I had been proceeding without thought of caution, for I was sure that the city and the palace were both in the hands of my friends by this time.

And so it was that I bolted into the chamber full into the midst of a dozen nobles of the court of Salensus Oll. They were passing through on their way to the outside world along the corridors we had just traversed.

At sight of us they halted in their tracks, and then an ugly smile overspread the features of their leader.

"The author of all our misfortunes!" he cried, pointing at me. "We shall have the satisfaction of a partial vengeance at least when we leave behind us here the dead and mutilated corpses of the Prince and Princess of Helium.

"When they find them," he went on, jerking his thumb upward toward the palace above, "they will realize that the vengeance of the yellow man costs his enemies dear. Prepare to die, John Carter, but that your end may be the more bitter, know that I may change my intention as to meting a merciful death to your princess—possibly she shall be preserved as a plaything for my nobles."

I stood close to the instrument-covered wall—Dejah Thoris at my side. She looked up at me wonderingly as the warriors advanced upon us with drawn swords, for mine still hung within its scabbard at my side, and there was a smile upon my lips.

The yellow nobles, too, looked in surprise, and then as I made no move to draw they hesitated, fearing a ruse; but their leader urged them on. When they had come almost within sword's reach of me I raised my hand and laid it upon the polished surface of a great lever, and then, still smiling grimly, I looked my enemies full in the face.

As one they came to a sudden stop, casting affrighted glances at me and at one another.

"Stop!" shrieked their leader. "You dream not what you do!"

"Right you are," I replied. "John Carter does not dream. He knows—knows that should one of you take another step toward Dejah Thoris, Princess of Helium, I pull this lever wide, and she and I shall die together; but we shall not die alone."

The nobles shrank back, whispering together for a few moments. At last their leader turned to me.

"Go your way, John Carter," he said, "and we shall go ours."

"Prisoners do not go their own way," I answered, "and you are prisoners—prisoners of the Prince of Helium."

Before they could make answer a door upon the opposite side of the apartment opened and a score of yellow men poured into the apartment. For an instant the nobles looked relieved, and then as their eyes fell upon the leader of the new party their faces fell, for he was Talu, rebel Prince of Marentina, and they knew that they could look for neither aid nor mercy at his hands.

Talu took in the situation at a glance, smiling.

"Well done, John Carter," he cried. "You turn their own mighty power against them. Fortunate for Okar is it that you were here to prevent their escape, for these be the greatest villains north of the ice-barrier, and this one"—pointing to the leader of the party—"would have made himself Jeddak of Jeddaks in the place of the dead Salensus Oll. Then indeed would we have had a more villainous ruler than the hated tyrant who fell before your sword."

The Okarian nobles now submitted to arrest, since nothing but death faced them should they resist, and, escorted by the warriors of Talu, we made our way to the great audience chamber that had been Salensus Oll's. Here was a vast concourse of warriors.

Red men from Helium and Ptarth, yellow men of the north, rubbing elbows with the blacks of the First Born who had come under my friend Xodar to help in the search for me and my princess. There were savage, green warriors from the dead sea bottoms of the south, and a handful of white-skinned therns who had renounced their religion and sworn allegiance to Xodar.

There was Tardos Mors and Mors Kajak, and tall and mighty in his gorgeous warrior trappings, Carthoris, my son. These three fell upon Dejah Thoris as we entered the apartment, and though the lives and training of royal Martians tend not toward vulgar demonstration, I thought that they would suffocate her with their embraces.

And there were Tars Tarkas, Jeddak of Thark, and Kantos Kan, my old-time friends, and leaping and tearing at my harness in the exuberance of his great love was dear old Woola—frantic mad with happiness.

Long and loud was the cheering that burst forth at sight of us; deafening was the din of ringing metal as the veteran warriors of every Martian clime clashed their blades together on high in token of success and victory, but as I passed among the throng of saluting nobles and warriors, jeds and jeddaks, my heart still was heavy, for there were two faces missing that I would have given much to have seen there—Thuvan Dihn and Thuvia of Ptarth were not to be found in the great chamber.

I made inquiries concerning them among men of every nation, and at last from one of the yellow prisoners of war I learned that they had been apprehended by an officer of the palace as they sought to reach the Pit of Plenty while I lay imprisoned there.

I did not need to ask to know what had sent them thither —the courageous jeddak and his loyal daughter. My informer said that they lay now in one of the many buried dungeons of the palace where they had been placed pending a decision as to their fate by the tyrant of the north.

A moment later searching parties were scouring the ancient pile in search of them, and my cup of happiness was full when I saw them being escorted into the room by a cheering guard of honor.

Thuvia's first act was to rush to the side of Dejah Thoris, and I needed no better proof of the love these two bore for each other than the sincerity with which they embraced.

Looking down upon that crowded chamber stood the silent and empty throne of Okar.

Of all the strange scenes it must have witnessed since that long-dead age that had first seen a Jeddak of Jeddaks take his seat upon it, none might compare with that upon which it now looked down, and as I pondered the past and future of that long-buried race of black-bearded yellow men I thought that I saw a brighter and more useful existence for them among the great family of friendly nations that now stretched from the south pole almost to their very doors.

Twenty-two years before I had been cast, naked and a stranger, into this strange and savage world. The hand of every race and nation was raised in continual strife and warring against the men of every other land and color. Today, by the might of my sword and the loyalty of the friends my sword had made for me, black man and white, red man and green, rubbed shoulders in peace and good-fellowship. All the nations of Barsoom were not yet as one, but a great stride forward toward that goal had been taken, and now if I could but cement the fierce yellow race into this sodality of nations I should feel that I had rounded out a great life-work, and repaid to Mars at least a portion of the immense debt of gratitude I owed her for having given me my Dejah Thoris.

And as I thought, I saw but one way, and a single man who could insure the success of my hopes. As is ever the way with me, I acted then as I always act—without deliberation and without consultation.

Those who do not like my plans and my ways of promoting them have always their swords at their sides wherewith to back up their disapproval; but now there seemed to be no dissenting voice, as, grasping Talu by the arm, I sprang to the throne that had once been Salensus Oll's.

"Warriors of Barsoom," I cried, "Kadabra has fallen, and with her the hateful tyrant of the north; but the integrity of Okar must be preserved. The red men are ruled by red jeddaks, the green warriors of the ancient seas acknowledge none but a green ruler, the First Born of the south pole take their law from black Xodar; nor would it be to the interests of either yellow or red man were a red jeddak to sit upon the throne of Okar.

"There be but one warrior best fitted for the ancient and mighty title of Jeddak of Jeddaks of the North. Men of Okar, raise your swords to your new ruler—Talu, the rebel Prince of Marentina!"

And then a great cry of rejoicing rose among the free men of Marentina and the Kadabran prisoners, for all had thought that the red men would retain that which they had taken by force of arms, for such had been the way upon Barsoom, and that they should be ruled henceforth by an alien Jeddak.

The victorious warriors who had followed Carthoris joined in the mad demonstration, and amidst the wild confusion and the tumult and the cheering, Dejah Thoris and I passed out into the gorgeous garden of the jeddaks that graces the inner courtyard of the palace of Kadabra.

At our heels walked Woola, and upon a carved seat of wondrous beauty beneath a bower of purple blooms we saw two who had preceded us—Thuvia of Ptarth and Carthoris of Helium.

The handsome head of the handsome youth was bent low above the beautiful face of his companion. I looked at Dejah Thoris, smiling, and as I drew her close to me I whispered: "Why not?"

Indeed, why not? What matter ages in this world of perpetual youth?

We remained at Kadabra, the guests of Talu, until after his formal induction into office, and then, upon the great fleet which I had been so fortunate to preserve from destruction, we sailed south across the ice-barrier; but not before we had witnessed the total demolition of the grim Guardian of the North under orders of the new Jeddak of Jeddaks.

"Henceforth," he said, as the work was completed, "the fleets of the red men and the black are free to come and go across the ice-barrier as over their own lands.

"The Carrion Caves shall be cleansed, that the green men may find an easy way to the land of the yellow, and the hunting of the sacred apt shall be the sport of my nobles until no single specimen of that hideous creature roams the frozen north."

We bade our yellow friends farewell with real regret, as we set sail for Ptarth. There we remained, the guest of Thuvan Dihn, for a month; and I could see that Carthoris would have remained forever had he not been a Prince of Helium.

Above the mighty forests of Kaol we hovered until word from Kulan Tith brought us to his single landing-tower, where all day and half a night the vessels disembarked their crews. At the city of Kaol we visited, cementing the new ties that had been formed between Kaol and Helium, and then one long-to-be-remembered day we sighted the tall, thin towers of the twin cities of Helium.

The people had long been preparing for our coming. The sky was gorgeous with gaily trimmed fliers. Every roof within both cities was spread with costly silks and tapestries.

Gold and jewels were scattered over roof and street and plaza, so that the two cities seemed ablaze with the fires of the hearts of the magnificent stones and burnished metal that reflected the brilliant sunlight, changing it into countless glorious hues.

At last, after twelve years, the royal family of Helium was reunited in their own mighty city, surrounded by joy-mad millions before the palace gates. Women and children and mighty warriors wept in gratitude for the fate that had restored their beloved Tardos Mors and the divine princess whom the whole nation idolized. Nor did any of us who had been upon that expedition of indescribable danger and glory lack for plaudits.

That night a messenger came to me as I sat with Dejah Thoris and Carthoris upon the roof of my city palace, where we had long since caused a lovely garden to be made that we three might find seclusion and quiet happiness among ourselves, far from the pomp and ceremony of court, to summon us to the Temple of Reward—"where one is to be judged this night," the summons concluded.

I racked my brain to try and determine what important case there might be pending which could call the royal family from their palaces on the eve of their return to Helium after years of absence; but when the jeddak summons no man delays.

As our flier touched the landing stage at the temple's top we saw countless other craft arriving and departing. In the streets below a great multitude surged toward the great gates of the temple.

Slowly there came to me the recollection of the deferred doom that awaited me since that time I had been tried here in the Temple by Zat Arrras for the sin of returning from the Valley Dor and the Lost Sea of Korus.

Could it be possible that the strict sense of justice which dominates the men of Mars had caused them to overlook the great good that had come out of my heresy? Had they so soon forgotten the debt they owed me in releasing them from the bondage of their horrid belief? Could they ignore the fact that to me, and me alone, was due the rescue of Carthoris, of Dejah Thoris, of Mors Kajak, of Tardos Mors?

I could not believe it, and yet for what other purpose could I have been summoned to the Temple of Reward immediately upon the return of Tardos Mors to his throne?

My first surprise as I entered the temple and approached the Throne of Righteousness was to note the men who sat there as judges. There was Kulan Tith, Jeddak of Kaol, whom we had but just left within his own palace a few days since; there was Thuvan Dihn, Jeddak of Ptarth—how came he to Helium as soon as we?

156

There was Tar Tarkas, Jeddak of Thark, and Xodar, Jeddak of the First Born; there was Talu, Jeddak of Jeddaks of the North, whom I could have sworn was still in his ice-bound hothouse city beyond the northern barrier, and among them sat Tardos Mors and Mors Kajak, with enough lesser jeds and jeddaks to make up the thirty-one who must sit in judgment upon their fellow-man.

A right royal tribunal indeed, and such a one, I warrant, as never before sat together during all the history of ancient Mars.

As I entered, silence fell upon the great concourse of people that packed the auditorium. Then Tardos Mors arose.

"John Carter," he said in his deep, martial voice, "take your place upon the Pedestal of Truth, for you are to be tried by a fair and impartial tribunal of your fellow-men."

With level eye and high-held head I did as he bade, and as I glanced about that circle of faces that a moment before I could have sworn contained the best friends I had upon Barsoom, I saw no single friendly glance—only stern, uncompromising judges, there to do their duty.

A clerk rose and from a great book read a long list of the more notable deeds that I had thought to my credit, covering a long period of twenty-two years since first I had stepped the ocher sea bottom beside the incubator of the Tharks. With the others he read of all that I had done within the circle of the Otz Mountains where the Holy Therns and the First Born had held sway.

It is the way upon Barsoom to recite a man's virtues with his sins when he is come to trial, and so I was not surprised that all that was to my credit should be read there to my judges—who knew it all by heart—even down to the present moment. When the reading had ceased Tardos Mors arose.

"Most righteous judges," he exclaimed, "you have heard recited all that is known of John Carter, Prince of Helium—the good with the bad. What is your judgment?"

Then Tars Tarkas came slowly to his feet, unfolding all his mighty, towering height until he loomed, a green-bronze statue, far above us all. He turned a baleful eye upon me—he, Tars Tarkas, with whom I had fought through countless battles; whom I loved as a brother.

I could have wept had I not been so mad with rage that I

157

almost whipped my sword out and had at them all upon the spot.

"Judges," he said, "there can be but one verdict. No longer may John Carter be Prince of Helium"—he paused—"but instead let him be Jeddak of Jeddaks, Warlord of Barsoom!"

As the thirty-one judges sprang to their feet with drawn and upraised swords in unanimous concurrence in the verdict, the storm broke throughout the length and breadth and height of that mighty building until I thought the roof would fall from the thunder of the mad shouting.

Now, at last, I saw the grim humor of the method they had adopted to do me this great honor, but that there was any hoax in the reality of the title they had conferred upon me was readily disproved by the sincerity of the congratulations that were heaped upon me by the judges first and then the nobles.

Presently fifty of the mightiest nobles of the greatest courts of Mars marched down the broad Aisle of Hope bearing a splendid car upon their shoulders, and as the people saw who sat within, the cheers that had rung out for me paled into insignficance beside those which thundered through the vast edifice now, for she whom the nobles carried was Dejah Thoris, beloved Princess of Helium.

Straight to the Throne of Righteousness they bore her, and there Tardos Mors assisted her from the car, leading her forward to my side.

"Let a world's most beautiful woman share the honor of her husband," he said.

Before them all I drew my wife close to me and kissed her upon the lips.

spot."

"Perhaps," he said, "there can be but one verdict. No longer may John Carter be Prince of Helium"—he paused—"but instead let him be Jeddak of Jeddaks, Warlord of Barsoom?"

ABOUT EDGAR RICE BURROUGHS

Edgar Rice Burroughs is one of the world's most popular authors. With no previous experience as an author, he wrote and sold his first novel—*A Princess of Mars*—in 1912. In the ensuing thirty-eight years until his death in 1950, Burroughs wrote 91 books and a host of short stories and articles. Although best known as the creator of the classic *Tarzan of the Apes* and *John Carter of Mars,* his restless imagination knew few bounds. Burroughs' prolific pen ranged from the American West to primitive Africa and on to romantic adventure on the moon, the planets, and even beyond the farthest star.

No one knows how many copies of ERB books have been published throughout the world. It is conservative to say, however, that of the translations into 32 known languages, including Braille, the number must run into the hundreds of millions. When one considers the additional world-wide following of the Tarzan newspaper feature, radio programs, comic magazines, motion pictures and television, Burroughs must have been known and loved by literally a thousand million or more.